LOVE'S TIME

LOVE'S MAGIC BOOK 3

BETTY MCLAIN

Copyright (C) 2017 Betty McLain

Layout design and Copyright (C) 2019 by Creativia

Published 2019 by Creativia (www.creativia.org)

Cover art by Cover Mint

Edited by Marilyn Wagner

This book is a work of fiction. Names, characters, places, and incidents are the product of the author's imagination or are used fictitiously. Any resemblance to actual events, locales, or persons, living or dead, is purely coincidental.

All rights reserved. No part of this book may be reproduced or transmitted in any form or by any means, electronic or mechanical, including photocopying, recording, or by any information storage and retrieval system, without the author's permission.

This book is dedicated to everyone who believes that Love transcends time.

CHAPTER 1

"Miss, Miss are you alright?" The policeman leaned over the young woman. Someone had reported seeing a body under a bush in the park. When Officer Michaels arrived at the park, he heard the body give a low groan. He leaned over and touched the woman on the shoulder. She groaned again and rolled over.

Angelica blinked up at the officer and then around at her surroundings. She had no idea where she was or how she had arrived there.

The officer looked at the woman. She had a large bump on her head and her face and head had blood on them. She tried to get up and fell back on the ground with another groan. "Just lie still. You have a nasty cut on your head and it looks like you have lost a lot of blood," he said as he observed the blood on the ground around her. "There's an ambulance on its way. Just relax until it gets here."

The siren on the ambulance could be heard coming closer. Angelica closed her eyes and winced as if the noise was hurting her head.

Officer Michaels waved the paramedics over when they stopped.

"What do we have here?" asked one of the paramedics.

"It looks like a mugging," answered the officer.

The paramedics checked her blood pressure and looked into her eyes. Then they put her on the gurney to transport her to the hospital.

"Is she going to be alright?" asked Officer Michaels.

"It looks like she may have a concussion and blood loss. I think she'll be alright. They can give you more information at the hospital. You want to follow us in?" responded the paramedic.

"Yeah, let me call it in and I'll be right behind you."

They each headed for their vehicles and drove towards the hospital. The paramedics called ahead to the hospital and there were attendants waiting at the door when they arrived. They rushed the gurney into a room where they transferred the patient to the bed. The paramedics were leaving as Dr. Steel entered the room.

"What have we here?" Dr. Steel asked.

"She was found in the park. The officer said she was a possible mugging victim. She has a head injury and a possible concussion," one of the paramedics replied before leaving.

Dr. Steel went to the patient and shone his small flashlight in her eyes. She winced as if the light hurt her eyes. He turned the light to the side and began examining her head wound. "Clean this up and put a liquid bandage on it," he instructed the nurse.

"Yes, doctor," the nurse responded before starting to work on cleaning the head wound.

"I don't think it needs stitches," he mused to himself. "She definitely has a concussion. She will have to be watched and awakened often to be checked on. Do we have an ID on her?"

"According to her driver's license in her pocket, her name is Angelica Black," responded the nurse.

Dr. Steel stopped and stared off into space for a minute. He shook his head and stared back down at the patient. She had the appearance of Native American ancestry, with black hair and a shape to her face that was indicative of those particular genes he knew so well. Just then Angelica opened her eyes and stared at Dr. Steel.

"Who are you? Where am I?" she was starting to get agitated.

"It's all right," Dr. Steel said calmly. "You are in the hospital. You have a head injury and a concussion. You appear to have had an accident in the park. Can you tell me your name?"

"Angelica Black," she replied.

"Do you remember getting hurt?" Dr. Steel probed.

"Yes, I was in the park with a friend. He wanted me to invest in a business for him. When I told him I would have to check it out first, he got mad and shoved me. I fell and hit my head on the seat as I fell. I don't remember too clearly what happened after I fell. I vaguely remember he seemed afraid as he ran off. I managed to get up, but I was disoriented and I stumbled around when I was close to the bushes, I fell again and passed out. I don't remember anything else until I heard the policeman calling me."

"What was your friend's name" asked Dr. Steel.

"Laughing Elk," responded Angelica.

Dr. Steel looked up surprised. He knew Laughing Elk. He didn't know him very well, but he had seen him around and about the reservation. Laughing Elk was a good twenty years older than him

"You're sure it was Laughing Elk?" he asked.

Angelica looked surprised. "Yes, I've known him all of my life. It was definitely him."

Dr. Steel looked at Angelica's driver's license. He stared at her address. "This is where you live, at 2309 Stone Hollow? It is inside the reservation."

"Yes, it is. My mother, Shining Star, received the land from her parents. She and my father decided to build their home there. It was a very happy place until they were killed by a drunk driver when they were in town. They left the place to me, along with a trust fund set up by my father's dad."

Dr. Steel looked at Angelica hard. "I know the place. I also know that it has been deserted for the last twenty years, after the daughter, Angelica disappeared. There is no way you could be Angelica Black. She would be forty-five years old now. You can't be more than twenty-five."

Angelica stared at Dr. Steel in shock. "What are you saying?" she whispered. "What is the date?"

Dr. Steel looked at her enquiringly. "What date do you think it is?"

"When I went into the park, it was May 17, 1995," she replied.

"Today's date is May 18, 2015."

Angelica looked at him in shock. "That's not possible."

There was a knock at the door and Moon Walking came in from where she had been standing, listening at the door. She looked at Angelica and smiled.

"Grandmother, what are you doing here?" asked Dr. Steel.

"I came to welcome Little Flower home," she replied.

Angelica gave a pleased cry at seeing someone she knew. "Moon Walking?" Her voice was slightly hesitant, but excited. She knew this woman, but she was much older than Angelica remembered. What the doctor said was true. "It is so good to see a friendly face. How did you know I was here?"

"The spirits told me to come, that it was time for your return. I always knew you would be back. You were in the wrong time. The universe has put you where you belong." She came over to the bed and, leaning over, gave a big hug to Angelica. "Welcome home, Little Flower."

Angelica sniffed back tears. "I haven't been called Little Flower since my mom died," she said tearfully.

"Hello," Officer Michaels stuck his head in the door. He came into the room and over to Angelica. "I have been waiting to find out what happened to you. Can you tell me how you got hurt?"

Still in shock, and with no small amount of disbelief, she made a quick decision and answered. "I'm still not to clear on what happened, Officer." That was putting it mildly. "I know I was in the park sitting on the bench. I got up to leave and somehow my feet got twisted and I stumbled over something. When I was falling, I hit my head on the edge of the bench. I think I must have knocked myself out for a few minutes. When I got up, I was still woozy and disoriented. I stumbled around and I must have passed out again by the bushes. I don't remember anything else until I heard you calling to me, trying to wake me up. I want to thank you so much for helping me. I'm very grateful." She shot a look at the doctor, silently asking him not to contradict her story.

"So, there was no one else involved," probed Officer Michaels.

"No, just my clumsy self," Angelica replied.

"Could I get your name and address for my report?"

"Of course. My name is Angelica Black and I live at 2309 Stone Hollow."

Officer Michaels wrote down the information and took his leave.

Angelica saw Dr. Steel and Moon Walking watching her for an explanation, and she sighed. "It was an accident, and it happened a long time ago. Besides, it is not like anyone outside the reservation would believe me if I told them the full truth, and the reservation has always policed their own," Angelica observed, answering their unasked question.

Moon Walking smiled at her and patted her arm. "Yes, we do," she said. "Laughing Elk will go before the tribal elders to explain why he did not try to help you. He may not have meant to hurt you, but running away is not an acceptable reaction."

"No, it is not acceptable. You could have been much more seriously hurt. The exposure did not help. Laughing Elk has some explaining to do," Dr. Steel stated, forcefully.

"When will Little Flower be able to go home?" asked Moon Walking.

"Not until tomorrow. I am keeping her over night to keep an eye on her concussion. Besides, nobody has lived in her house in a long time," Dr. Steel observed.

Moon Walking smiled at Little Flower. "Your house is fine. The ladies have kept it aired and cleaned. Some of the boys have kept the yard work done. I knew you would be back and I wanted you to stay where you belong, with your mother's people."

Angelica felt tears forming in her eyes. She blinked to hold them back. "Thank you," she said simply.

"We are transferring Angelica to a room, Grandmother. Do you want to say good night and let her get some rest?" asked Dr, Steel.

"No, Running Wolf, I will accompany her to her room and stay the night. I do not want Little Flower to wake alone," Moon Walking said in a firm voice. Everyone knew when she used her firm voice, she wasn't budging.

Dr. Steel gave in gracefully. He allowed Moon Walking to follow as Angelica was moved to a room and they settled in for the night. Moon Walking leaned back and closed her eyes so Angelica could fall asleep without feeling guilty.

CHAPTER 2

Dr. Steel saved Angelica until last on his rounds to check on his patients the next day. When he entered her room, he had her discharge papers with him. He found Angelica and Moon Walking talking quietly. They both looked up with a smile when he entered the room.

"Are you ready to get out of this establishment?" he asked teasingly.

"Yes, please," responded Angelica.

"I have the paperwork here. As soon as you sign it, we can get going. The nurse said you were doing very well."

Angelica signed the papers and handed them back to Dr. Steel. "Now, if Moon Walking will help you get dressed, I will drive you both to the reservation." Dr. Steel looked at Moon Walking. "How did you get here from the reservation?"

Moon Walking looked at him blankly for a minute, then smiled. "I caught a ride with the postman."

Dr. Steel just shook his head. He knew the postman was not supposed to give rides when delivering mail, but nobody turned Moon Walking down when she asked a favor.

"Okay, I'll meet you at the nurse's desk as soon as you are ready." He turned and left the room.

Angelica lost no time in getting out of bed and reaching for her clothes.

Moon Walking stopped her with a touch on her arm.

"No, those clothes are torn and dirty. I brought you clean clothes." She opened the bag she had with her and pulled out one of Angelica's own dresses and some underclothes.

Angelica gasped. "How did you know I would need these? Never mind, stupid question. Thank you, Moon Walking, I was not looking forward to wearing those old clothes. She quickly got dressed and they went out to find Dr. Steel.

Dr. Steel was watching for them and, when he saw them coming, he came to meet them with a wheelchair.

Angelica frowned at the chair. "I don't need to ride in a wheel chair. I can walk."

"Hospital rules, everyone being discharged has to be taken out in a wheelchair. Come on. It won't hurt a bit. We will soon have you outside at my car." Dr. Steel declared, cheerfully.

Angelica reluctantly sat in the chair and allowed herself to be pushed out to the car.

Dr. Steel had asked one of the interns to move his car to the exit, so it was waiting outside as they came out of the door. When they were in the car and on the way to the reservation, Dr. Steel looked at Angelica. He had buckled her into the front seat and Moon Walking was in the back seat.

"My name is Alex," he told Angelica.

Angelica smiled. "Pleased to meet you, Alex. Dr. Steel does get to be a mouthful when you keep saying it."

"So does Running Wolf," replied Alex.

"I like Running Wolf," said Angelica.

"It is a fine name. I picked it out for your mother," replied Moon Walking, from the back seat.

"Yes, Grandmother, it is a fine name. Thank you for picking it out for me." Moon Walking grunted with satisfaction.

It wasn't long before they were pulling up into the drive of Angelica's house. Alex opened the back door for Moon Walking and hurried around the car to help Angelica. Angelica had her seat belt off and was opening her door when he got there. Alex took her hand and helped her from the car.

Angelica stood staring up at her house before she started toward the front door. She didn't say anything until she reached the door.

"I guess I have a key here somewhere," she said, looking in her purse.

"You do not need a key," said Moon Walking. "It's not locked."

Angelica looked startled. "Why not?" she asked.

"It was easier for the ladies to come in and keep things clean and fresh. No one would dare to break into a house under my protection," declared Moon Walking.

"No, they wouldn't," agreed Alex as he reached around Angelica and pushed the door open.

Angelica stood just inside and looked around, wide eyed. "It looks just like I just stepped out a few minutes ago," gasped Angelica.

"I told everyone that you would be back and to keep everything ready for you," said Moon Walking.

Angelica sniffed back a couple of tears. She then turned to Moon Walking and gave her a hug.

"Thank you so much," she said. "I was dreading coming back here after I found out I had been gone for twenty years. I was afraid it would be falling down around me. This is fantastic."

"I will leave you to get settled in," said Moon Walking. "I need to check on things in the village."

"Just a minute and I will give you a ride," said Alex.

Moon Walking looked at him sternly. "I don't need a ride. These two feet have been taking me wherever I need to go for a long time. They will continue to do so."

Alex raised his hands. "I'm sorry, I didn't mean anything by offering a ride. I was just trying to be helpful."

Moon Walking's expression softened. "I know," she said, smiling. "Why don't you stay and help Little Flower settle in. Let me know if she needs anything. I need to set up a meeting of the tribal elders for Laughing Elk. I will let you both know when it is, so you may attend."

Alex's expression hardened. "Good, I have a few words I need to pass on to him."

After seeing Moon Walking out, Alex turned to Angelica. "Is there anything you need help with?" he asked.

Angelica shook her head as she slowly looked around.

"I can't believe how well taken care of everything is." She turned and went into the kitchen. Alex followed her. Angelica went over and opened the refrigerator. Tears came to her eyes again. She blinked rapidly to keep them from falling.

"What's wrong?" asked Alex.

"The refrigerator is full of food," sniffed Angelica.

Alex smiled. "Did you really think Moon Walking would miss a detail like having a well-stocked refrigerator? That would be one thing she would be sure to take care of. If there is anything else you need, just let me know, and I will be sure you get it. I don't want you going to the store or anywhere else for a couple of days. Things have changed quite a bit. It will all take some getting used to, I would imagine. I will check on you tomorrow to see how you are doing." Alex took a card out of his pocket and handed it to Angelica. "This has my cell phone number on it. I can be reached on it anytime. Now, I want you to get into bed and rest for today. I will wait until you have gotten into bed, and then I will leave." He held up his hand as Angelica started to protest. "Doctor's orders," he said.

Angelica sighed and turned to do as he instructed. She looked back at Alex. "I am going under protest," she said smiling at him. "Thank you, Alex for taking care of me."

"You're welcome," said Alex, smiling back.

Angelica turned and entered her bedroom.

CHAPTER 3

Angelica awoke the next morning feeling much better, but she was still a little stiff. After taking a nice warm shower, she wandered into the kitchen to find something to eat. She didn't see anything she wanted, so she decided to make some pancakes. She had gathered a bowl and the ingredients to make the pancakes on to the table when there was a knock at the door. Angelica put down the spoon she was holding and went to answer the door. She opened the door and smiled widely at Moon Walking. "Hello, Moon Walking. How are you this beautiful day?"

"I am doing well," said Moon Walking. She followed Angelica toward the kitchen.

"I am making myself some pancakes. Would you like to join me?" asked Angelica.

"That would be very nice. I stopped by to tell you about the meeting of the tribal elders. It is going to be tomorrow night."

"They are moving fast," said Angelica, surprised.

"Yes, I told them I wanted the matter resolved quickly," replied Moon Walking. "You and Running Wolf will be called to answer questions."

Angelica paled. "I don't want to cause any trouble."

"You will not be causing trouble. You will only tell the truth."

"Does Laughing Elk have a family?" asked Angelica.

"Yes, he has a son and a daughter. His wife died five years ago. His daughter is living with his sister. His son is nineteen. He is in his first year at the university."

Angelica thought about everything and continued making her pancakes. She did not want to disrupt Laughing Elk's life. He did not mean to hurt her. True enough, he could have gotten help for her, but he was young and scared, and maybe he had tried to get help, but she was gone when he returned. She had no way of knowing. Angelica finished her pancakes and placed them on the plates. She put syrup and butter on the table along with two cups of coffee, placed the sugar bowl and creamer on the table and turned to get the plates of pancakes, only to find Moon Walking already placing them on the table. "Let's eat," she said, smiling at Moon Walking.

They sat down and bowed their heads for a brief prayer. "These are very good," said Moon Walking, after savoring the first bite.

"Thank you," said Angelica. "It was one of my mom's favorite meals to make. She taught me how to make them when I was six years old. We always enjoyed making them together."

After they finished eating and clearing the table, Moon Walking prepared to leave. "Running Wolf will come by and take you to the meeting of the tribal elders. Do not worry. They will not be too harsh with Laughing Elk. Everything will be all right." She patted Angelica on the arm and left.

Angelica wandered around and looked at things. She picked up the picture of her mom and dad. She blinked back tears as she looked at them. They looked so happy. That drunk driver took a happy family and tore it apart. Angelica returned the picture to the shelf with a sigh. She decided to see what she had to wear to the meeting with the tribal elders. She looked for something comfortable but classy.

Angelica found a tan dress with designs worked around it with beads. She also found her moccasins and tried them on. They fitted perfectly. The strings went around her legs and tied in front. Angelica admired the way they looked before taking them off and laying them with her other clothes for the next day.

Angelica hurried to answer the door the next day. She was already wearing her tan dress and moccasins. "Hi, Alex," she greeted, smiling.

"Wow, you look great," said Alex. He gave her a long look and smiled back at her. "Are you ready to go?"

"Yes, just let me grab my purse and key." Angelica turned to a small table and got her purse. She went out and locked her door. When she put the key in her purse she turned to Alex with a smile.

Alex hurried to open the door of his car for her. Once he had her tucked in, with seat belt fastened, he hurried around to the driver's side and got in. It was a short drive to the meeting hall. They were soon pulling into a parking space and exiting the car. Alex took Angelica's arm and escorted her inside. The inside of the room was large and there were chairs on one side. Three of the chairs were occupied by very elderly Indian men. Moon Walking occupied a chair to one side of the elders. She motioned for Alex and Angelica to join her.

When they reached her side, she stood and took Alex and Angelica each by the hand and guided them to the front of the elders.

"Black Bear, Grey Squirrel, and Smiling Beaver, you remember my grandson, Running Wolf," she paused as each of the elders acknowledged Running Wolf. "This is Little Flower the daughter of Shining Star." She motioned toward Little Flower.

"It is good to see you returned to us, Little Flower," said Black Bear. The other two nodded their agreement.

"Thank you. It is good to be home," said Little Flower.

Moon Walking guided Running Wolf and Little Flower back to their chairs and they all sat down.

The door opened and Laughing Elk entered. His face paled when he spotted Little Flower sitting in the group. He came forward and lowered his head respectfully to the group of elders. He did not say anything. He waited for them to speak first. Black Bear looked at him sternly. "Laughing Elk, you may be seated. We will hear the charges against you and then you may speak." Laughing Elk nodded and turned, then sat down.

Black Bear turned his head and motioned for Little Flower to come forward. "Little Flower, will you tell us what happened on the day you were taken from us."

"Yes," agreed Little Flower. "I was in the park with Laughing Elk. Laughing Elk asked me to finance a business he was interested in. I told him I would have my accountant look over the deal and let him know later. Laughing Elk must have thought I was turning him down. We were standing by a park bench, and he shoved me. I stumbled around and fell. When I fell, I hit my head on the bench and passed out. When I came to, I got to my feet, but I was very disoriented. I stumbled over to some bushes and I passed out again. When I awoke, a policeman was standing over me and he called an ambulance to take me to the hospital. It was then that I found out that it was twenty years later."

Little Flower lowered her head and waited for Black Bear to speak. "Thank you, Little Flower. You may sit." Little Flower went back to her chair and Black Bear turned to Laughing Elk and motioned for him to come forward. Laughing Elk came forward and waited to speak. "Do you have anything to add to the story told by Little Flower?" asked Black Bear.

"It happened as she said. I did not mean to hurt her. When she fell there was so much blood, I thought she was dead. I got frightened and ran off. I came back later, but she was gone and I could not find her. I didn't know what to do, so I did nothing."

Black Bear stared at him thoughtfully. "You do know there will be a payment made for your cowardliness. Are you prepared to accept our judgment?"

"Yes, I am," responded Laughing Elk.

Black Bear looked toward Moon Walking, Little Flower and Running Wolf. "Are there any suggestions?" he asked.

Running Wolf stood and faced the elders. "If I may make a suggestion," when the elders nodded, he continued. "Laughing Elk has dishonored the name given to him. I think his name should be changed to Stripped Weasel to show his dishonor." Running Wolf took his seat and waited for the elders' reaction to his suggestion.

Black Bear and the others talked quietly amongst themselves. When they finished with their discussion, Black Bear motioned for Laughing Elk to come forward.

"Will you accept the name change?" he asked.

Laughing Elk looked at Little Flower and quickly looked away. "Yes," he replied.

"Very well, from now on you will be known as Stripped Weasel. This meeting is over."

Black Bear and the others rose and left the meeting room. Moon Walking turned and started to say something to Little Flower, but was interrupted by Stripped Weasel. "Little Flower, I just wanted to say I am glad you are alright," he said.

"Thank you," replied Little Flower. Stripped Weasel turned and left.

"Are you ready to go, now?" asked Running Wolf.

"Yes, please. Thank you, Moon Walking for taking care of everything," she squeezed Moon Walking's hand and smiled at her.

Moon Walking patted Little Flower's hand. "You two go on. Running Wolf, you take good care of Little Flower. We have to make sure she stays with us." Moon Walking turned and left them standing there.

"What do you think she means? Is there a chance I may return to the past?" she looked at Running Wolf inquisitively.

Running Wolf shook his head and took Little Flower's hands in his. "I do not know. I hope not. I like having you around." Little Flower smiled at Running Wolf. "Let's go, I have something I want to ask you about."

They left the meeting hall and went out to Alex's car. When they were in the car, Angelica turned to Alex. "You know it is easy to think of you as Running Wolf at the meeting hall, but as soon as we are away from there you become Alex again." She shook her head.

"I know," agreed Alex. "You were Little Flower there, and now you are Angelica again." Angelica and Alex smiled at each other in understanding.

"What did you want to ask me about?" enquired Alex.

"I wanted to ask you about my driver's license. It expired long ago and the birth date on it makes me forty-five. I don't know how I will ever be able to get it renewed. I need to be able to drive since I live so far out of town." Angelica twisted her hands together as she waited for Alex to answer. Alex reached over and placed a hand over hers. She instantly stilled and looked at him.

"We can take care of it tomorrow. It is too late today. I will be by after my rounds at the hospital to take you to see Yellow Hawk. He is in charge of issuing driver's licenses on the reservation. He can tell us what we need to do. Do not worry. He will believe you. It would be a different story if you had to go into town to get your license. The reservation takes care of its own, you know," he smiled, reminding her of her words at the hospital. "Everything will be alright. You'll see." He squeezed her hand and then returned his hand to the steering wheel as he turned into the drive of her house.

Alex helped Angelica from the car and walked her to the door. She turned to face him and smiled. "I am taking a lot of your time. Thank you for helping me."

"I am glad to help," Alex leaned closer and placed a gentle kiss on her lips. He pulled back and looked to see if she objected to his forwardness. Angelica continued to smile at him. He gave a sigh of relief. "I will see you tomorrow. Let's get you inside." He took her key, opened the door and ushered Angelica inside. He placed another gentle kiss on her lips and said good night as he left.

Angelica placed her fingers on her lips and smiled. She stood and savored the nice feelings Alex left her with. As she went to prepare for bed, she knew it was going to be a good night. She was sure to have good dreams. Angelica thought about Laughing Elk, no Stripped

Weasel, she corrected herself. She hoped he didn't suffer too many repercussions from the name change, but the punishment could have been much worse, and it was done now.

Returning to her previous thoughts of Alex, she hugged herself, turned out the light, and snuggled into bed.

CHAPTER 4

*A*lex hurried through his rounds the next day. He did not deny attention to any of his patients, but he did not linger and talk to them as he sometimes did. As soon as he was finished, he turned in the charts and left the hospital.

He went by his house first to change out of his hospital clothes. He thought Angelica should have another view of him outside his doctor image. When he entered his car, he called Angelica.

"Hello," answered Angelica.

"Hello, this is Alex. I wanted to let you know I will be on my way to your house in a few minutes."

"I'll be ready," she answered.

"I talked to Yellow Hawk. He said for you to bring your driver's license and your birth certificate. I have some more information from Moon Walking, but I'll tell you about it when I get there."

"Alright, I'll see you soon," agreed Angelica.

Alex knocked on her door about ten minutes later. "Hi."

He was greeted with a smile as Angelica opened the door. "Hi," said Angelica smiling back at him. They stood staring at each other for a minute. Alex leaned forward and kissed her gently.

"Oh my, you seem to be making a habit of doing this," said Angelica softly.

"Do you object?" asked Alex just as softly.

"No," said Angelica shaking her head.

"Good," said Alex.

"Come in," said Angelica, letting him in and shutting the door. "You said you had some more news."

"Yes," agreed Alex. They both took a seat on the sofa and Angelica looked at Alex expectantly.

"Moon Walking has already talked to Yellow Hawk. They have everything arranged between the two of them. He will fix you up when we see him. She also talked to one of the directors at your bank. He just happens to be the son of Black Bear. He has been taking care of your trust fund and your bank accounts. Moon Walking told everyone you would be back and to keep everything in order for your return. Little Bear has kept records of all of your accounts and he is ready to turn them over to you as soon as we go by his office at the bank. So, we need to get to the bank and the driver's license place. Are you ready?"

"Yes, I'm ready. I have my license and my birth certificate in my purse," she replied, standing.

Alex took her hand and led her to his car. After helping her into the car, he entered the driver's side and started the car. Alex looked at Angelica and saw she was looking a little tense. He reached over and patted her hand. "Don't worry. Everything will be alright. You'll see."

They arrived at Yellow Hawk's office and knocked on the door. When a voice called, "Come in," Alex opened the door and ushered Angelica inside.

"Hello, Morning Star," Alex greeted the young lady at the desk. "This is Little Flower we are here to see Yellow Hawk. Little Flower, this is Morning Star. She is a cousin of yours on your mother's side of the family."

"Hello," replied Little Flower and Morning Star together.

"It will be nice to get to know some of my family." Angelica smiled. Morning Star smiled back and agreed.

Yellow Hawk stuck his head out of his office. "Hello, I thought I heard Running Wolf's voice out here."

He came out to shake Alex's hand and turned to Angelica with a smile. "This must be Little Flower. I am glad you are back with us. Moon Walking assured us all you would be returning." He offered his hand to her. Little Flower shook his hand with a smile. "Now if you both will come into my office and let me get everything straightened out."

They both followed him into his office after giving Morning Star a smile. Little Flower took out her birth certificate and driver's license and handed them over to Yellow Hawk.

He took the items and studied them. "This will not be a problem," stated Yellow Hawk. "On your birth certificate, I will change your birth date from 1970 to 1990. Your parents will not have their dates changed. They only have their age on here not their birth date. So the only one changing is you. Your driver's license is the same. We will just change your birth date from 1970 to 1990."

He pulled up the program on his computer and made the corrections. "Now if you will stand in front of the camera and sign the license, we will have it ready in a few minutes."

He showed her where to sign and where to stand. He quickly snapped her picture. While the license was processing, he went to work on her birth certificate. He printed out a copy and stamped it so it would be certified. There was a ding signaling the license was ready. Yellow Hawk retrieved the license and birth certificate and presented them to Little Flower.

"Welcome home, Little Flower," he said as he handed them to her.

"Thank you. I really appreciate you making this so easy for me. What do I owe you for these?" she inquired.

"These are on the house. Moon Walking would never let me hear the end of it if I charged anything. We all want to stay on Moon Walking's good side." He exchanged a look of complete understanding with Running Wolf.

They said goodbye to Yellow Hawk and Morning Star as they left.

When they were in the car and on their way, Angelica looked at Alex. "I hope the bank is as easy as this. I need to get everything straightened out so I can use my money."

Alex patted her hand. "I am sure Moon Walking has paved the way for us," he said, smiling.

Angelica smiled back at him. "She has really been taking care of me. I owe her a lot." She looked away thoughtfully. When she looked back at Alex, she seemed hesitant.

Alex looked at her pryingly. "Is something wrong?" he asked.

"I was wondering. Is there something the reservation needs but has put off getting because of funds?"

"I don't know. I will have to think about it. I am more involved with the hospital than tribe business. I will find out and let you know."

"Thanks," replied Angelica.

They pulled up into the parking lot of the bank. They sat looking at it for a minute. "It looks almost the same as it did twenty years ago," said Angelica.

"I guess some things, like banks, enjoy their image enough to stay the same. Come on, let's go inside."

They exited the car and Alex took her hand as they went inside. They followed the signs until they found Derrick Bear's office. Alex knocked on the door. The door was opened by a man who had a startling resemblance to Black Bear. When he saw them standing there, he smiled and ushered them inside.

"We are all glad you are alright and have returned to us, Little Flower. Is it alright if I call you Angelica? I need to explain your accounts to you."

"Yes, please do," replied Angelica.

Derrick Bear smiled. "I have already changed your birth date to 1990. Moon Walking instructed me to fix the date about a week ago."

"A week ago!" exclaimed Angelica. "I have only been back 4 days." Derrick and Alex smiled. "Okay, I get it. Moon Walking knew I would be back," Angelica sighed.

Derrick just smiled and pulled forward some papers. "You will find everything in order. I have ordered you new checks, a debit card and a credit card. You just need to put your signature on these papers. He handed her a couple of papers to sign. Angelica looked them over and signed them. Derrick took the papers from her and put one in her pile and one in the bank's pile.

"You will find the trust fund is worth about six times what it was when you left us. The Black Foundation, started by your grandfather, is doing very well and is being run by a board of trusties. You are quite a wealthy young woman. Do you have any idea what you are going to do now?"

"Well, I am planning to spend some on the reservation. I just need to see where it is most needed. I am also going to look for a part time job, something in the art field. I majored in art at college and I am not going to sit around and just spend money."

Derrick looked thoughtful. "Moon Walking can help you decide where the money is most needed on the reservation. I also heard the art gallery is looking for part time help. You might go by and talk to them. Don't rush yourself. Enjoy being home for a few days first."

"I will," agreed Angelica, rising from her chair.

Derrick put all of her papers into a folder and handed them to her. "If there is anything I can help you with, just give me a call. My card is in the folder. I will be glad to help any way I can."

"Thank you," said Angelica.

Derrick and Alex shook hands and Alex guided Angelica out of the bank.

Alex turned to Angelica. "Would you like to get an ice cream cone while we are in town?"

Angelica smiled. "I would love to. Can we leave these papers in your car?"

"Sure," said Alex. He took the papers and put them in the back seat of the car. After locking the door, he took Angelica's hand and they strolled down the street toward the ice cream parlor.

They walked slowly. Angelica was looking around to see the changes in stores. Some of the old stores were gone and there were a lot more specialty stores. She was glad the old ice cream parlor had survived. She had a lot of fond memories of it. Her dad and mom would take her by to get a cone on Sundays after church. She sighed. She really missed them. They had been gone a long time, but it didn't seem like such a long time to her.

They arrived at the ice cream parlor. Alex opened the door and ushered her inside. There was a line of people waiting for ice cream. Alex and Angelica went to the end of the line and patiently inched their way to the counter.

"What can I get for you?" asked the teenager behind the counter.

"I'll have a chocolate and vanilla swirl," stated Angelica, smiling at Alex.

"I'll have strawberry banana swirl," stated Alex.

They received their cones and went to a table to sit and enjoy them.

After taking the first lick on the cone, Angelica sighed with pleasure. "This is so good," she said. "Would you like a taste?" she asked Alex. She held the cone toward him so he could taste it.

"Ummm, good," said Alex. "Would you like a taste of strawberry banana," he asked, holding his cone out to her.

"Yes, please," replied Angelica. She leaned forward to take a taste. She sighed with pleasure. "Next time I will have to try this."

Alex smiled as he continued to lick his cone. "This is one of my favorite places. I always try to stop by when I am in town."

"It is one of my favorite places, also. My parents used to bring me here on Sundays, after church. I'm glad it has survived."

When they finished their cones, they threw away their trash and walked back outside. Alex reached for Angelica's hand and pulled her closer to his side. Angelica smiled and stayed close to him. They looked around and Angelica spotted Mason's Art Gallery about a half a block away on the other side of the street.

"Is that the art gallery Derrick was talking about?" she asked, pointing at it.

Alex looked up the street at the art gallery. "Yes, it is the only art gallery in town. Would you like to look around?"

"Could we? I don't want to take up too much of your time," she looked at Alex enquiringly.

"I have plenty of time. I finished my rounds and I am not on call, so I am at your disposal. We can do whatever you want."

"You had better watch making statements like that. You never know how much trouble it could get you into." Angelica smiled up at Alex.

Alex smiled back at her and squeezed her hand. "I meant every word," he said. "Come on let's go see the art gallery."

CHAPTER 5

As they casually strolled down the street, several people called out to Alex, calling him Dr. Steel. He would wave to acknowledge them, but did not stop. He continued to focus his attention on Angelica. He was pointing out new stores and some old ones. He did not want the outside world to intrude on his time with Angelica.

All at once, he let go of her hand and stood in front of two teenagers coming toward him on skateboards. He held up his hand to signal them to stop. Both boys stopped when they saw him. Alex looked at them sternly before speaking. "Little Oak and Grey Pony, why are you out and about instead of in school?"

"School was dismissed early. Moon Walking said they needed to decorate the building for a welcome home party for Little Flower. She sent me and Grey Pony to pick up some streamers from the flower store," Little Oak explained patiently.

"I see," said Alex.

"We have to go, Running Wolf. Moon Walking doesn't like to be kept waiting." Grey Pony was anxious to be on his way.

"Alright, you two be careful and don't run over anyone," said Alex.

"We are always careful," declared Little Oak. With a wave the boys were on their way.

"Did you know Moon Walking was planning a party?" querried Angelica.

"No, she hasn't gotten around to telling me, yet." Alex reached for Angelica's hand and they started walking toward the art gallery again.

As they entered the art gallery, the bell over the door tinkled merrily. "I like the sound. It sounds so happy," said Angelica.

"Hello," called a voice. "I'll be right there." The lady came out of the back room and came to greet them, smiling. She stopped when she spied Alex.

"Dr. Steel," she said smiling and extending her hand to Alex. Alex shook her hand, but looked puzzled about her identity. "I'm Melanie Mason," she explained. "I want to thank you for taking care of my daughter, Valerie, when she was stung by the bee."

"I had help from Marcus. How are Valerie and Marcus doing?"

"They are doing great. It is wonderful to see my daughter and Marcus so much in love and planning their wedding," Melanie sighed. "It is a lot of work, though. They are going to be married in a month here in Rolling Fork at our church. We couldn't have it outside because of the bees. The reception afterward will be at the country club. I know Valerie is inviting you. She wanted to invite your grandmother, Moon Walking, but she didn't know where to send the invitation."

"Moon Walking will like that. Tell Valerie to send it to the reservation. Moon Walking will get it. Everyone knows her." Alex smiled at Melanie and turned to Angelica. "Melanie, this is Angelica Black. Melanie's daughter, Valerie was a patient of mine. She is very allergic to bee stings and the medicine usually used to treat the stings. Marcus was able to let me know which medicine to give her. It all worked out in the end, but it was close."

"It must have been scary for your family," Angelica said to Melanie.

"It would have been, if I had been here. My husband and I were on a trip to Italy at the time. By the time we found out, it was all over. Listen to me," she said apologetically. "I'm keeping you here talking instead of seeing what I can help you with. Is there anything in particular you are interested in?"

"Yes," said Angelica. "I see you have a help wanted sign in the window. What kind of help do you need?"

"Well," said Melanie smiling. "I mainly need someone to cover the front room and talk to customers. Cindy works the back room and my husband handles the book work. I usually handle the front, but I need to take time off to work on Valerie and Marcus' wedding. Do you think you would be interested?"

"Yes, I would like some part time work. I have a degree in liberal arts, but I don't have any experience. I am a fast learner, though."

"How many hours a day do you think you could work?" asked Melanie.

"I could do 4 hours a day. I can't work on Sunday." She looked at Melanie expectantly.

"How about we start you off tomorrow and see how it works for the rest of the week. We can talk more after we see how you do. Is that okay with you?" Melanie asked.

"I'll be here tomorrow. What time do you need me?" Angelica had a big smile on her face. She looked at Alex excitedly.

"We open at nine. If you could get here at eight thirty, we can fill out paperwork and I can show you around. Just come to the back door and knock and someone will let you in. Welcome aboard, Angelica." Melanie held out her hand for Angelica to shake. Angelica shook her hand and turned to Alex.

"I can't believe it," she said giving him a hug. "I have a job."

"So, I see," said Alex, smiling and hugging her back. "We had better go so you can prepare for tomorrow. It was nice to see you," he told Melanie. "Please tell Valerie and Marcus hello for me."

"I will," agreed Melanie. She watched as Alex and Angelica started back up the street toward their car. "Another couple in love," she mused. "There must be something in the air lately."

"I thought you were going to wait a few days before getting a job," remarked Alex.

"I was, but I couldn't resist asking," Angelica said happily.

"If you start feeling tired, you rest. Melanie will understand. She is a very nice person."

Angelica stared at Alex curiously. "I didn't think you knew her when we entered the store."

"I didn't, but I know her daughter and Marcus. They are very nice people and Valerie talked about her mother and father a lot. She missed them even though she was falling in love with Marcus. You are going to their wedding with me, aren't you?" Alex requested.

"Are you sure they won't mind?" asked Angelica.

"They will probably not see any one else but each other," said Alex with a smile.

They had made it back to the car. Alex opened the door and ushered Angelica inside before climbing into the driver's side.

"Do you need to get anything while we are in town?" he asked.

"No, I can't think of a thing. We need to find out when Moon Walking is having her party," Angelica said.

"Yes, I had almost forgotten about that. We had better go find out what is going on."

Alex started the car and headed for the reservation.

Alex pulled up in front of the school house and turned to Angelica. "You should wait here for me. I don't know if Moon Walking is planning the party to be a surprise. I'll go and see what I can find out."

"Okay," agreed Angelica.

Alex got out and went inside. Angelica looked around curiously. The building looked good. It was in good repair. She frowned. They needed a large gym to use when it was raining. There were kids scattered around using outside sport setups.

Some were playing basketball. There was a soccer field and a baseball diamond. There was a small playground for the younger children. Angelica looked around. There was a large vacant lot on the east side of the school. "I wonder if that could be used for the school," she thought. She turned back, facing front as Alex emerged from the building. She smiled at him as he slid into the car.

Alex smiled back and reached over to squeeze her hand. "The party is tonight at six o'clock. I told grandmother you could only stay a couple of hours because you needed your rest. She agreed with me and asked me to bring you. She also wanted to know if we had got everything straightened out. She said to tell you that you will enjoy working at the art gallery."

"What! Did you tell her about the job?" asked Angelica.

Alex shook his head. "Nope, not a word. She always knows."

Angelica shook her head and laughed. "I bet it was rough growing up around her. She knew you were headed for trouble before you even did anything."

Alex looked at her and laughed with her. "Yeah, we didn't get away with anything."

Alex parked his car in Angelica's driveway. He hurried to help her out and escort her to her door. After Angelica opened the door, Alex pulled her close and gave her a gentle kiss. As he felt her responding, he deepened the kiss. After a minute he pulled back and laid his forehead against hers. Neither of them was out of breath, but they were breathing hard.

Alex looked down into her eyes. "Try to get a nap. I'll pick you up at five thirty. We don't want to be too late. Moon Walking might send someone after us." He laughed softly.

Angelica smiled up at him. "I'll try," she promised. Alex kissed her once more, gently, and turned to go. "Alex," called Angelica. Alex turned to see what she wanted. Angelica walked out toward him. When she stood in front of Alex, she stopped and looked up at him. "You could stay here. We could sit and talk, or we could watch television." She sighed. "I just don't want to be alone."

"Okay, I would love to sit and relax with you," he replied. Alex took her hand and they turned and entered the house together. Angelica led the way to the sofa and pulled on Alex's hand for him to sit, also.

"Would you like anything to drink?" she offered.

"No, I'm fine. I just want to sit here and talk and get to know you better. You must have guessed I have feelings for you. I know this must seem sudden, but I feel like we have grown close and packed a lot into a few days."

"Yes," agreed Angelica. "I feel very safe when I am with you. I feel like the universe sent me into the future so I would be able to meet you on equal footing."

Alex squeezed her hand, leaned forward and placed a gentle kiss on her lips. When he started to pull back, Angelica reached up and held the back of his head so the kiss could continue and deepen. When they finally parted lips, they both leaned their heads so their foreheads were touching and both were breathing heavily. Angelica smiled at Alex and lay her head on his chest. "Do you mind if we just sit here like this for a while?" she asked.

Alex tightened his arm around her and whispered. "I would love to sit here like this for as long as you will let me."

Angelica smiled and snuggled closer to Alex. Her eyes closed and she was soon sleeping. Alex smiled and kissed the top of her head. He was very careful not to jostle her. She needed a nap. He was very happy to be sitting there holding her.

CHAPTER 6

Angelica stirred and opened her eyes. She looked around and, when she realized where she was, lay very still. She looked up at Alex, who had fallen asleep holding her in his arms. She smiled. She had never felt so safe and protected. Even though she had really only known Alex a few days, she was beginning to develop strong feelings for him. It made her feel giddy, just lying there in his arms.

Alex stirred and opened his eyes. He smiled at Angelica, when he saw she was awake and watching him.

"I guess I must have dozed off," he said.

"I think we were both in need of a nap," replied Angelica.

Alex tightened his arms around her briefly, but when he looked at his watch, he sighed. "I'm going to have to go. I need to get home to shower and change for the party tonight."

Angelica sat up and stretched. "Yeah, me too. I have no idea what to wear. What does one wear to a surprise welcome home party?" she asked.

Alex smiled and pulled her close for a kiss. "It doesn't matter what you wear. You always look beautiful." He stood and, pulling Angelica with him, headed for the front door. At the door he turned her to face him and kissed her again. "I'll see you in a little while," he said.

"Okay," agreed Angelica. She closed the door behind Alex and hurried to her room to decide on her outfit for the party. She looked in her closet. There was an extensive wardrobe to choose from. She looked around and spied a royal blue dress. It was fitted at the top and had a slightly flared bottom. The flared skirt would make walking and sitting easier. She lay the dress on the bed and started gathering accessories to go with it.

After she had picked out everything to go with the dress, she headed to the bathroom to take a shower. She was showered, dressed and just finishing her makeup, when she heard a knock at the door. She took one last look in the mirror and went to let Alex in.

"You look beautiful," Alex declared in a choked voice. "How do you manage to look more beautiful each time I see you?"

Angelica smiled up at Alex. "You are looking handsome. I don't think I have seen you in a suit before. You wore hospital clothes at the hospital and casual clothes when we went to town. I definitely approve," she said.

Alex leaned toward her, then stopped. "Will it mess up your lipstick if I kiss you?" He asked.

"No, it is smudge proof," Angelica smiled and offered her lips for a kiss.

Alex lost no time in obliging her. He kissed her gently, then, held her closely for a moment before pulling back. "I guess we have to go," . Angelica smiled as he took her hand. He helped her into his car and fastened her seatbelt before entering the driver's side and starting the car.

Alex had to look for a place to park when they arrived. The school parking lot was full of cars. When he found a spot, they had a long walk, weaving in and out of cars, to reach the front door. When Alex opened the door for Angelica, the sound blasted out at them. Angelica grabbed Alex's hand and held on tightly. Alex put his arm around her and leaned in closely.

"It's alright. I should have warned you about the sound," he said.

"I'm fine. Just for a minute it reminded me of the parties I attended when my parents were alive."

Alex squeezed her closer. He spotted Morning Star making her way toward them. Morning Star stopped in front of them and leaned in to give Angelica a hug. "I didn't get a chance to talk to you in Yellow Hawk's office. I just wanted to say that I am glad to meet you and I hope we can be friends." She smiled at Angelica.

"I hope so, too. I was thinking about you after we left the driver's license office. Didn't your family live in Canada?" asked Angelica.

"Yes, we moved down here about fifteen years ago. Mom was very upset about Shining Star's death. Dad thought it might be better if we moved down here. Come on, I'll introduce you to her, Grandma and Grandpa Star."

"I have a Grandma and Grandpa?" enquired Angelica.

"Yes," replied Morning Star. She kept a determined path through the crowd. Angelica and Alex followed closely behind her to keep from being separated. Morning Star came to a stop in front of an elderly couple and a lady about her mother's age. She bore a striking resemblance to Angelica's mother.

"Grandma, Grandpa, Mom, this is Little Flower. Little Flower this is Grandma, or Red Night Star, Grandpa, or Dancing Star, and my mother, Shooting Star." She stood back smiling and waited for someone to speak.

Shooting Star rose from her chair and approached Little Flower. "We are so very glad to meet you. We are glad you were returned to us." She leaned over to give Little Flower a hug.

Little Flower hugged her back and smiled mistily. "I am glad to meet all of you. Mother told me about all of you. I'm sorry we didn't get a chance to meet before now."

She walked over and gave her Grandma and Grandpa a brief hug. We are going to have to get together and get to know each other, but I need to go and find Moon Walking and thank her for putting together this welcome home party for me. I will see all of you later." Little Flower gave them all a smile and turned to Alex.

"Do you know where Moon Walking is?" she asked.

"Yes, she is over by the band." Alex shook hands with her Grandpa and Grandma and gave Shooting Star a kiss on the cheek.

"We'll catch up with you all later," he promised.

They watched the band as they made their way to Moon Walking. There were two guitar players, a fiddler, and someone playing drums. The music sounded nice. Angelica thought it would sound better if it wasn't quite so loud. Just as they reached Moon Walking, the band started their break. Moon Walking stopped them as they lay their instruments down and left the stage.

"Little Flower, this is the Leopard family. They have been making music for our tribe for a long time. Little Leopard and Double Leopard are twins and they play the guitars." She motioned to the two guitar players and Angelica smiled and shook hands with the two. "The drums are played by Dark Leopard and their father, Spotted Leopard, plays the fiddle. Spotted Leopard is also the school principle." Angelica shook hands with the last two and told them she enjoyed their music. The guys all left to get refreshments and Angelica and Alex turned to Moon Walking.

"Thank you for arranging this party for me," said Angelica. She gave Moon Walking a hug and smiled at her. "I have just met some of my relatives. I look forward to getting to know them better." Angelica smiled at Moon Walking again.

"I thought the best way to let everyone know you were home was to get them all together at once and let them see for themselves," said Moon Walking. "It will be good for you to get better acquainted with your family."

"Yes, it will," agreed Angelica. She looked at Moon Walking with a big smile. "I have a part time job. I start tomorrow at the art gallery. Also, I want to talk to you about where I need to donate money to help the reservation. I know you will know where it is needed most." Angelica looked at Moon Walking seriously.

Moon Walking patted her hand. "We will get together in a few days and discuss it. Tonight, just enjoy the party. You and Running Wolf go and dance. The band is about to start playing again."

Angelica looked around at the stage. She had been so engrossed in talking to Moon Walking, she hadn't noticed the band returning. She hugged Moon Walking again and, turning to take Alex's hand, she let him guide her out to where there were some people dancing. Alex turned her around, and they joined the line of dancers. It was slow and Angelica soon became comfortable with it. She just had to remember the moves from when her parents brought her to similar dances.

Angelica looked at the other dancers. Morning Star was dancing with Derrick Bear. She smiled and waved at both. They both smiled and waved back. Yellow Hawk was dancing with a pretty girl. She had not seen her before. At least, not that she could remember. Alex tugged on her hand to bring her attention back to him. He leaned close and whispered in her ear.

"You have plenty of time to get to know everyone. Be patient."

Angelica smiled at him and squeezed his hand. When the dance came to an end, Alex looked up and saw three young men heading toward them. He gave them a hard look. Two of the men saw the look and turned away. They did not want to tangle with Running Wolf. The other man kept coming. He had known Running Wolf all of their lives and was not intimidated. He came to a stop in front of Running Wolf and Little Flower.

"Hello, I'm Lone Wolf. Running Wolf is my cousin," he smirked at Running Wolf. "Would you like to dance?"

Angelica smiled at him and looked at Alex. She was unsure what she should do. He looked steadily back at her, leaving it up to her. Angelica shook her head and looked back at Lone Wolf.

"No, thank you, but I am with Running Wolf," she answered.

Lone Wolf backed away and Alex and Angelica stood holding hands and staring into each other's eyes. Angelica smiled and Alex smiled back. They were in perfect accord with each other.

Moon Walking watched them from over by the band. She looked

satisfied to see how well Little Flower and Running Wolf were getting along. "They make a fine couple," she thought. "They will make me a nice group of great grand babies." She sighed again with satisfaction.

Alex and Angelica stayed another hour. They greeted a lot of people and mingled with the crowd. Angelica spent some time talking with her grandparents and her aunt. She promised to get in touch as soon as she knew what hours she would have free from her new job. She said goodnight to them and she and Alex made their way back to Moon Walking.

"We came to say good night," said Alex, kissing her cheek.

"Yes," agreed Angelica. "We had a great time. Thank you so much for arranging everything." Angelica leaned in and gave her a big hug.

"You two go along," she said. "Have a good rest and we will get together soon and have a nice long visit. Maybe over breakfast," she added, and Angelica laughed.

"You know you are welcome to come to breakfast anytime," said Angelica.

They all said good night again and Alex and Angelica walked toward the door. Once outside, Alex and Angelica headed for where they left the car. The crowd had thinned out some as people left the party for home. When Alex had Angelica buckled in and they were on their way home, Alex reached over and took her hand.

"I had a great time tonight. Thank you for going with me," he said.

"I had a great time, too. Thank you for taking me," Angelica smiled at Alex, even though he couldn't see her very well in the dark.

When they arrived at Angelica's house, Alex walked to the door and opened it for her. Inside the door Alex drew her close and kissed her. When he pulled back, he cupped her face gently in his hand. He looked in her eyes for a moment and, with a sigh, he rested his forehead against hers.

"I have to go. We both have to go to work tomorrow. Call me when you are finished. We can get together and grab a bite to eat." He kissed her again softly and held her closely for a minute. He pulled away reluctantly and headed out of the door. He looked back at Angelica, standing there looking after him.

"Come, lock the door," he said.

Angelica went to do his bidding and locked the door. She heard Alex's car start up and heard him leaving. She turned with a smile and headed for the stairs. She hugged her happiness to her as she sang softly. Her life was coming together nicely. She also had a wonderful man interested in her. She had some relatives to get to know and she had a job.

Angelica set her alarm clock before lying down. She did not want to be late on her first day.

CHAPTER 7

The phone woke Angelica from a sound sleep early the next morning. She fumbled around her bedside table and located her phone.

"Hello," she whispered.

"Hello," answered Alex. "I'm sorry if I woke you. I just wanted to say good luck on your first day at the art gallery. I wanted to call you before I left for the hospital."

"Alex, what time is it?" Angelica looked around for her clock. She located it on the floor by the bed. She must have knocked it off when the alarm went off.

"It's 6:30," Alex replied.

"Oh, I am so glad you called. I must have turned the alarm off and gone back to sleep. I am also glad for a chance to say good morning, too."

"Good morning. You have plenty of time. Just take a deep breath. You will be fine. Call me when you get off work. You promised to go out to eat and we can celebrate your first day at work." Alex smiled hopefully to himself.

"I would like to celebrate with you," agreed Angelica with a smile of her own. "I had better get up and start to get ready. Thanks for calling. You helped to start my day off right."

"Talking to you is the best way to start my day, too, except for holding you and getting an early morning kiss. I had better get to the hospital. I'll see you later," Alex hung up the phone reluctantly. He gave a huge sigh, but nothing could wipe the smile off his face. Angelica was meant for him and he was going to make sure nothing and no one stopped them from being together.

Angelica was also smiling as she hung up the phone. She hurried into the kitchen and started the coffee maker running while she took a shower and got dressed.

By the time she had showered, dressed and eaten a bagel with cream cheese on it, which she enjoyed with a cup of fresh brewed coffee, it was 7:30. Angelica decided to go ahead and get started for the art gallery. She didn't know how the traffic would be. She would rather be early instead of late. It was 8:10 when she pulled into a parking spot to the side of the gallery. She went to the back door and knocked as Melanie told her to do.

The door was opened by a young woman. She smiled at Angelica and motioned her inside so she could close the door.

"Hi," she said and offered her hand. "You must be Angelica. Melanie told me to expect you. I'm Cindy."

"Yes, I'm Angelica," Angelica shook her hand and gave her a big smile in return.

"Melanie and Frank haven't made it yet, but they will be here soon. Come on I'll show you the most important room in the gallery," said Cindy laughing. She led the way to the break room. Both girls laughed as they entered the room.

"I can see why it could be very important," agreed Angelica.

"It can be a real life-saver sometimes," Cindy stated with another smile.

The back door opened and they heard voices coming closer. Melanie and her husband entered the break room. Melanie laughed. "I can see Cindy has already shown you our most important room," she extended her hand to Angelica and turned to face her husband. "This is the young lady I was telling you about. Angelica, this is my husband Frank Mason. Frank say hello to our newest employee, Angelica Black."

"Hello, Angelica. It's nice of you to join us at the gallery. I hope you will like working here." He extended his hand and smiled at Angelica.

Angelica shook his hand and smiled back. "I'm sure I will, Mr. Mason."

Frank shook his head. "Call me Frank. We are very informal here. I think you will fit right into our family. I have some work I have to see to," he said turning to Melanie. "I'll see you later, dear." He turned and, with a wave, headed for his office.

After Frank left, Cindy took her coffee cup to the sink and turned to go. "I have some stock to unpack, so I will see you later. Angelica, welcome aboard," Cindy replied.

"Thank you. I'm sure I will be happy here," Angelica replied.

Melanie smiled at Angelica. "Are you ready to get started?" she asked.

Angelica stood and joined her at the door. "All ready," she agreed.

Melanie led the way. She briefly opened the door to the back room where Cindy was working. "This is where everything is catalogued before it is placed on the floor for sale."

She closed the door without bothering Cindy. She continued on down the hall. "This next room is Frank's office. On the other side of the hall is the wash room and restroom. You have already seen the break room." She continued through the double doors into the main part of the gallery. "Cindy does most of the displays. She has a great eye for placing things to show them to their best advantage. The cash register is over behind the counter and we have a nook over by the side for people to sit and have some tea or water. It's a new addition and has turned out to be very popular. Most of the articles in the gallery have a code stamped on the bottom. When they are run through the scanner it tells you how much they cost."

"What a neat idea," said Angelica.

Melanie looked at her strangely. "Haven't you seen a scanner before?" she asked.

"No, I haven't. Like I told you, I haven't had a job before, but I am a quick learner," Angelica told her seriously. She was afraid the job offer might be withdrawn.

Melanie patted her hand. "We will have you up to speed in no time at all," she replied. "Come on I'll show you how to run the cash register."

She led the way over to the counter and explained its points to Angelica. "Don't worry. If you get stuck or need help, I'll be here today. I'll help until you get more comfortable with everything."

"Thank you," said Angelica.

The bell over the door sounded as the first customers of the day entered. Angelica smiled as the two elderly ladies came in and headed for the area with tea and water.

Melanie greeted them by name and turned to introduce them to Angelica. "Angelica, these ladies are two of our best customers. They have been visiting us since we opened the gallery. This is Sally Reynolds and Grace O'Malley. Ladies, this is Angelica Black. She has agreed to join our gallery family." The ladies and Angelica all smiled and said hello.

"If there is anything I can help you with, just let me know," said Angelica.

The ladies agreed and took their tea with them as they started to look around. They talked in low voices to each other as they wandered around. After r a while, they came toward the cash register. Each had found an angel figurine to buy. Melanie had stayed close by so she could help Angelica, if she needed help. Angelica took the first figurine and scanned it as Melanie had shown her.

"Are these separate or together?" she asked.

"Ring them up together," said Sally. "We'll settle up with each other later." She smiled at Grace, who answered with a smile of her own.

Angelica scanned the other figurine and told them the total. Sally took out her debit card and swiped it through the machine next to the cash register. She put her pin number in and then punched the enter button. Angelica looked at the cash register. It said "Accepted, Sale Complete," and printed out a receipt. She tore the receipt off and handed it to Sally.

"Thank you for shopping at the gallery," she said with a smile. The ladies took their bag and, leaving their cups on the counter, walked out of the front door.

Melanie laughed. "Those two always leave their cups on the counter. You did very well." She assured Angelica. Melanie picked up the discarded cups and headed for the break room to leave them to be washed.

Angelica sighed and smiled with satisfaction. She survived her first sale. She was going to like this job.

When Melanie came back to the front, she brought some papers with her. She gave them to Angelica. "These are the papers I told you about. You can fill them out when you have time and give them back to me before you leave. There is not a lot to them. It is mostly name, address, social security number and dependents."

"Okay," agreed Angelica. "I'll get them filled out." Since no customers were in the store, she opened the papers and started filling them out. As Melanie told her, the papers were not complicated and she soon had them finished. She took the papers to Melanie.

"That was quick," said Melanie.

"Yes, it was as you said, very simple," agreed Angelica.

Melanie took the papers and headed for the office.

"I'm going to help Cindy in the back for a while. If you need help, just call." She smiled and left after Angelica agreed.

The bell over the door rang. Angelica looked toward it as two more ladies entered. One was middle aged and one looked to be a teenager. You could tell their native heritage by looking at them.

"Hello," Angelica greeted them with a smile. "If you need any help just let me know." The ladies smiled back, but didn't say anything as they continued to look around. The younger girl kept stealing glances at Angelica. Whenever Angelica looked at her, she would look away quickly. The older of the two found an item and headed for the cash register. She laid the item, an enameled snuff box, on the counter and waited for Angelica to ring it up.

Angelica started to scan the article. She glanced at the younger girl. She was startled to see tears in her eyes. "Is something wrong?" she probed.

The older lady looked at the younger one and sighed.

"I'm sorry. Little Elk has been upset ever since she found out about her father's name change. She doesn't want her name changed. The other children are teasing her about it. Seeing you made her think about it, and she is young, she does not control her emotions very well."

"Is she Laughing Elk's daughter?" Angelica pried.

"Yes. I am his sister, Standing Elk. Is there any way the children can keep their names? Do their names have to be changed with their father?"

"I don't know, but I will find out." She smiled at Little Elk. "I will let you know as soon as I know anything."

"Thank you," said Little Elk, shyly. The ladies took their package and left the gallery.

"Moon Walking, I need you," thought Angelica.

"I will see you at your house after work," Moon Walking replied in Angelica's mind. Angelica looked around startled. She shook her head. Now she was hearing things.

She was soon busy. She had a steady stream of customers all morning. At 12:30 Melanie came to relieve her.

"You have done very well. Every time I peeked in here, you were busy. I guess everyone wanted to check out the new girl. We will see you tomorrow. Have a good rest." Melanie walked her to the back door and let her out. She locked the door behind her.

Angelica drove home. She was tired, but it felt good. She was happy with all she accomplished. She was not surprised to see Moon Walking waiting in her porch swing. Angelica hurried from her car to the porch. She gave Moon Walking a hug and sat down beside her.

"Tell me what is so urgent," said Moon Walking.

"Will Stripped Weasel's daughter and son have to change their name to match their father's name?"

Moon Walking looked thoughtful. "You met Stripped Weasel's daughter?" she enquired.

"Yes, she was very upset."

Moon Walking sighed. "There is no need for her to be upset. I will talk to her. The childrens' names will not be changed. Stripped Weasel's name change is not permanent. It was to teach him a lesson. The council thought it would have more impact if he did not know it only lasted three months."

Angelica smiled. She gave a big sigh of relief.

"I'm glad. I am so happy. I don't want anyone else to be unhappy."

CHAPTER 8

Angelica looked at Moon Walking enquiringly. Moon Walking looked back at her and smiled. "Is there anything wrong?" she asked.

"Well, I was just wondering about something," answered Angelica.

"What's that?" asked Moon Walking, patiently.

"When I was at the gallery, after I talked to Laughing Elk's daughter. I was thinking about needing to talk to you. I thought I heard you answer me in my head." Angelica paused and looked at Moon Walking expectantly.

Moon Walking smiled at Angelica. "Of course you heard me, just as I heard you when you called to me. I have always had this ability and it seems you have it also. You could hear other people with practice. It is a very convenient thing to have." Moon Walking smiled at Angelica and gently patted her hand.

"I don't know if I want to be listening to other people's thoughts, except maybe for Alex. It might be nice to be able to communicate with him that way." Angelica shook her head thoughtfully.

Moon Walking laughed softly. "Yes," she agreed. "Being able to hear a lover's voice is very nice."

Angelica looked startled. "We aren't lovers," she protested.

Moon Walking patted her hand again and smiled. "You will be," she assured Angelica. She walked towards the door. When Angelica got over her astonishment at Moon Walking's last statement, she hurried to see her out and to say good bye.

Angelica called Alex as soon as Moon Walking was gone. She had promised to call him when she left work, but she had wanted to talk to Moon Walking first.

"Hello," answered Alex.

"Hello," said Angelica.

" Have you just finished work?" asked Alex.

"No, I needed to talk with Moon Walking. She was waiting for me when I arrived home." Angelica paused for a moment, waiting for Alex to speak.

"Are you still ok to go out? You aren't too tired?" Alex paused. He was waiting for Angelica's answer.

"I'm not tired at all. I can't wait to see you." Angelica assured Alex.

Alex gave a sigh of relief. "I missed you. It seems like forever since I held you in my arms. I'll be over in about twenty minutes. I have to check one more patient, and then I'll be there."

Angelica smiled. "I'll be waiting." She hung up the phone and hurried to change out of her work clothes.

When Alex arrived, Angelica hurried to open the door for him. She nestled into his arms and he pulled her close and kissed her. She deepened the kiss and kissed him back. Angelica finally pulled back and took a deep breath. Alex held her closely and tried to get his breath under control, also. He leaned back slightly and looked her over,

"You look very beautiful," he whispered. He pulled her close again. "Do you have any idea what kind of food you would like to have tonight?"

"I don't care," answered Angelica. "I just want to share it with you."

"There is a café on the reservation. It serves authentic Indian cuisine." Alex smiled down at her face and leaned in for another brief, kiss.

Angelica sighed. "That sounds like a good idea. I haven't had any authentic Indian food in about twenty years," she said with a laugh.

Alex laughed with her. "Ok," he agreed. "Let's go see what's cooking."

He reluctantly turned her from his arms and guided her out to the car. It was not very far to the café. The parking lot had a good amount of cars, but was not over crowded. Alex found a good parking spot and helped Angelica from the car. He held her hand as he guided her to the café. There were a lot of greetings from the people sitting at the tables. Alex waved and nodded to most of the people, but he didn't stop to talk as he guided Angelica to a table. They sat and waited while the waitress took their order and hurried off to get their drinks.

"How did your first day at work go?" asked Alex.

"It was fun," said Angelica, excitedly. "I learned a lot. Everyone was very nice to me. I am so glad I found the job. It is perfect for me."

Alex smiled at her enthusiasm. "I think it is perfect for you, also," he agreed.

They sat, gazing into each other's eyes until they were interrupted by the waitress with the food. Everyone seemed to sense they wanted to be alone, so they weren't bothered. They enjoyed the food and each other. Angelica looked at her watch. She gave a sigh when she saw how long they had been sitting, eating and talking.

"We are going to have to go. I need to get some sleep so I can get up in the morning. I don't want to turn off the alarm again," she laughed softly.

"Yes," agreed Alex. "I know you need your rest, but I don't mind being your alarm clock. It starts my day off better, just talking to you." He squeezed her hand and looked deeply into her eyes.

Alex got up and put some money on the table before going around the table to help Angelica up. They smiled and waved to a few people as they left, but they didn't linger to talk. After a make out session inside Angelica's front doorway, Alex reluctantly said goodnight and left. Angelica hugged her feelings closely and went upstairs to prepare for bed. The phone rang as she lay down.

"Hello, Alex," she answered.

"How did you know it was me?" asked Alex.

"Who else would it be?" she asked. She smiled slightly.

"I just wanted to say good night," Alex responded.

"Good night, Alex," she whispered. "I miss your arms around me."

"Me, too," said Alex. "I'll call you in the morning. Good night."

They both, reluctantly, hung up and turned to try and sleep.

The next days were busy for Angelica, but she enjoyed her job very much. Melanie was trusting her more and began taking some time off to work on Valerie and Marcus' wedding preparations. The time was getting close for the wedding and they were all getting excited. Angelica offered to help, but Melanie assured her that, by keeping everything going at the gallery, she was being a big help.

Angelica and Alex were spending every moment together they could. When Alex was free from the hospital, the first thing he did was call Angelica. They spent a lot of time at Alex's house and at Angelica's house. They wanted to be alone to get to know each other better. The make out sessions were sometimes hot and heavy. Other times they just sat on the couch and held each other while talking.

Moon Walking came by Angelica's house several times. She and Angelica were working out the details on a new sport complex for the young people to use during and after school. The project was coming along well and Angelica was very pleased with it. It was to be dedicated to her mother and it was to be called The Shining Star Sport Complex.

Finally, the plans for the complex were ready and the ground breaking was in two days. Alex was taking the day off from the hospital to be there and Angelica told Melanie she needed the day off to attend. Angelica was surprised when Melanie and Frank decided to attend the ground breaking.

"You are part of our family," said Melanie. "Of course we will be there." She gave Angelica a hug. "It's a great thing to be able to help young people. I know your mom would be very proud to have her name on the new complex."

"I think so, too," said Angelica. Her eyes were watery from holding back tears.

Melanie gave her another hug and hurried away to work on wedding plans.

Angelica smiled and turned to help a customer.

CHAPTER 9

The day arrived for the ground breaking. The tribal elders were there, as were the mayor and town council from Rolling Fork. The newspaper was represented and a lot of people from the community were there. Angelica's grandparents, aunt, and many cousins were there. When Angelica and Alex arrived, they made their way to the dig site. Someone handed Angelica a shovel. She looked at it and then looked at Alex.

Alex smiled. "The first shovels of dirt are symbolic."

Everyone was looking at Angelica as if they expected her to say something. Moon Walking came over and patted her shoulder for encouragement. Angelica cleared her throat. "Hello, everyone, I want to thank you all for being here today to support the building of The Shining Star Sports Complex. I know my Mom would be very proud to see something, to help the young people, named after her. So, in the name of Shining Star and for all of the native community, I am turning the first shovel of dirt."

Angelica dug in her shovel and tossed the first one. The others standing around quickly added their shovels of dirt to the site. They all started coming around and shaking Angelica's hand and thanking her for helping the community.

Angelica smiled at everyone and thanked each one for coming. When Frank and Melanie came by, she hugged each of them and thanked them for coming. She was glad to see the crowd clearing out. She turned to Alex and Moon Walking and smiled.

"Would it be alright to leave now?" she asked.

Moon Walking squeezed her hand and agreed they could leave. The three of them started walking toward Alex's car. When they arrived at the car, Moon Walking said she had something to take care of and left them. She gave both Angelica and Alex a hug when leaving.

"I think Moon Walking approves of us being together," said Alex. "She is looking really pleased with herself."

"She's just happy with the new complex. She worries about the young people on the reservation. Life can be rough on them, sometimes," said Angelica.

"Yeah, I know," agreed Alex. "I still think she is pleased to see us together."

"So am I," said Angelica. "I am very happy we found each other."

"Me, too," agreed Alex. He reached for Angelica's hand and gave it a squeeze. "You have the rest of the day off. Would you like to try out the Bantam Rooster Restaurant in the mall?"

"That sounds like fun," agreed Angelica. "I have never been there, but I overheard some girls talking about it when they were shopping at the gallery. They had good things to say about the restaurant."

"It's a nice place," agreed Alex. "Let's go check it out."

He pulled into the mall parking lot and found a place close to the restaurant. He helped Angelica out of the car and held her closely as they made their way into the restaurant. Alex spotted an empty table next to a window and led Angelica over to it.

They had only just sat down when the waitress came to their table. "Hello, Dr. Steel. What can I get for you?" she asked.

"Hello, Dianne. We are going to have some gumbo and iced tea. Is that okay with you?" he asked, turning to Angelica.

"Yes, I have wanted to try the gumbo ever since I heard about it," agreed Angelica.

"Coming right up," said the waitress, as she left to get their order. The waitress was back in a very short time. She had a tray with two large bowls of gumbo and two glasses of tea.

"You all enjoy your meal," she said, as she left.

"Thank you. We will," said Alex, as he and Angelica started to eat their gumbo.

"Oooh, this is good," said Angelica, savoring the taste of the gumbo.

"Yes, it is," agreed Alex, as he dug into his own bowl. They didn't talk much as they savored their meal.

Angelica sat back with a sigh. "I couldn't eat another bite," she said. "It was so good. I made a pig of myself." She gave a small laugh.

Alex smiled with her. He leaned back in his chair also. "I know what you mean. I am stuffed. One reason I don't come here too often is I don't want to stop eating. Sometimes there is a long line of people waiting to get in here. The gumbo is very popular." Alex replied.

"I can see why," agreed Angelica.

"Are you ready to go? We can walk around the mall and let our food settle," said Alex.

"I like looking around the mall," said Angelica, enthusiastically.

Alex put some money on the table and took Angelica's hand. They strolled around the mall, looking at displays and studying different stores. There were quite a few stores Angelica had never seen before.

"I still have a lot to learn about this time," she remarked.

"It will come. There is no hurry," Alex assured her. "I'm here for you any time you need help or don't understand something."

Angelica snuggled closer to Alex. She felt so safe when he was near.

They walked around a short time more and then decided to go to Angelica's house and watch a movie.

When they arrived at Angelica's house, Angelica went to pop some corn and get some iced tea. Alex went to a bag of movies he brought from home and started looking through them. When Angelica came in with their popcorn and tea, she looked curiously at the movies. Alex had some of them spread out on the table in front of the sofa.

Angelica smiled at the collection. "You must watch a lot of movies," she said.

"Some," said Alex. "I have been collecting these for years. Is there anything in particular you like to watch?"

Angelica sat down the popcorn and tea and started going through Alex's stack of movies. Alex reached into the large bowl of popcorn and helped himself to a handfull. "Umm, this is good," he said as he savored it.

Angelica smiled and handed him a movie. "I think this one might be good," said Angelica.

Alex looked at the movie Angelica was holding out to him. It was the Princess Bride. "Okay," he agreed.

Alex put the disc into the player and turned on the television. He returned to the sofa and sat down next to Angelica. He arranged the popcorn and tea where each of them could reach everything, then settled back on the sofa, putting his arm around Angelica, and turned on the movie.

As the movie came to an end, Angelica leaned back closer to Alex and sighed. "I really enjoyed the movie," she said to Alex.

"I could tell," he said with a laugh. "I thought a couple of times you were going to start telling the actors to stop messing around and get on with it."

Angelica laughed. "I can get pretty emotional about my movies."

"I didn't mind," said Alex. "I like to see you emotional. It's refreshing. A lot of girls these days hide their feelings. You don't know what they are feeling or thinking."

"Well," said Angelica. "I might hide my feelings from other people but never from you."

Alex leaned in for a kiss. Angelica was ready for this kiss. She had been anticipating it for a while. She snuggled closer and kissed him back. They kissed for several minutes. They only stopped briefly to breathe. They were just getting into another kiss when Alex's pager buzzed.

Alex leaned back with a sigh. He pressed his forehead to Angelica's for a minute. "I have to check in. The hospital wouldn't call me if it wasn't important," he said with a sigh.

"I know." said Angelica.

Alex took out his cell phone and called the hospital. After talking with them, he hung up and pulled Angelica close. "There has been a bad accident out on the highway. Some teens were drag racing and there was a pile up. The hospital is calling everyone in. I have to go," Alex hated leaving Angelica.

"Of course you do. Call me when you can and go save some lives," Angelica urged Alex toward the door. She leaned in for another kiss as he left.

Angelica leaned back against the locked front door. She sighed. This is the life of an important doctor she thought. Oh well, Alex was worth all the interruptions. She went to clean up the living room and put away the movie.

CHAPTER 10

The next day, Angelica was looking out the front window of the gallery when a chauffeur-driven car pulled up in front of the store and stopped. The chauffeur got out of the car and hurried to open the rear door. The other rear door opened as if the person was impatient with waiting. An older woman got out of the side with the chauffeur and a young woman and man got out by themselves.

The older woman spoke briefly to the chauffeur and he turned to leave. Then all three turned and started walking toward the gallery.

The two younger ones were holding hands and walking close to each other. It was as if they couldn't stand not touching. The young woman smiled up at the man. It was beautiful to see. Angelica could see how very much in love these two were.

The young woman smiled as she entered the gallery and looked around.

"Where is everyone?" she asked.

"Melanie and Cindy are working in the back room," said Angelica.

Before anyone could say anything else, Melanie and Cindy erupted from the back room. "Valerie!" exclaimed Melanie. She hurried over to give her daughter and Marcus a hug. Cindy welcomed Valerie warmly. Melanie then turned to the older lady and embraced her also.

"Emily, I am so glad they brought you along," she said.

Valerie laughed. "Actually, she brought us in her limo."

Melanie laughed. "Well, I am glad you are all here. We only have two more weeks to the wedding and I could use your input on the arrangements."

"Mom, I know you have everything in fabulous order. I am not worried about that. I just wanted to see you and Dad. Where is Dad?" she asked.

"He's in his office. I'll go get him. Before I go, I want you to meet Angelica. She has become an important member of the gallery family. You two talk while I get your dad," said Melanie. Valerie went over to Angelica and gave her a hug. Startled, Angelica hugged her back.

"Thank you so much. I am so glad you are working here so Mom has time to work on my wedding. I have been worried she might have been overdoing it. She told me what a big help you have been," Valerie said earnestly.

"I enjoy working here. Everyone is so nice to me," said Angelica.

"Well, of course they are. They love having you around. You fit right in," Valerie assured her.

"Valerie," called Frank as he came from his office.

"Hi, Dad," said Valerie going forward to give her Dad hug.

Marcus came forward to shake Frank's hand and say hello. Frank spotted Emily and went to greet her, also.

"Hello, Emily," said Frank. "How do you like your stay in Denton?"

"I like it," stated Emily. "I have met some very nice people. They have made me feel right at home. Dana helped me find a house. It's a lovely place. As soon as I get settled, I intend to have you and Melanie over for a visit."

"Melanie would like that. I know she misses spending time with you," Frank said as he turned back to Valerie.

"How long are you staying?" Frank asked.

"We are going to be here overnight. Marcus only has a couple of days off." Valerie smiled at Marcus and squeezed his hand. Marcus smiled back and pulled her closer to his side.

Melanie came in from the back room. She had a stack of books in her arms. She came up to Valerie and Marcus.

"Do you want to look at these here or go somewhere else to look at them? We could go over to the coffee house and get some coffee and a sweet roll while you see what I have arranged," Melanie was determined to get Valerie and Marcus to look at what she had organized.

Valerie laughed. "Okay, Mom. Lead the way." Valerie, Marcus, Emily, and Frank all followed Melanie out the door and across the street to the coffee house.

Angelica smiled as she watched them go. They were all enjoying the planning and excitement of the wedding. A customer came in and Angelica got back to work. She really liked working in the gallery.

The group settled around a large table. It had plenty of room for Melanie to spread out her books and show Valerie and Marcus the arrangements she had made. Emily leaned in closely and studied them. Frank sat back and smiled indulgently. Valerie beamed around the table at everyone. She was so happy and so in love. She squeezed Marcus' hand and smiled at him. Marcus squeezed back and smiled, also.

"Do you like these flowers?" asked Melanie. "There are a lot of spring colors and I thought they went very well with your color scheme."

"I love them," said Valerie. "They will go with everything and look bright and cheerful. Don't you think so, Marcus?" Valerie turned to get Marcus' opinion.

"I love them," said Marcus. "Are they for decorating the church?"

"Some are for the church and some for the country club. I ordered plenty," said Melanie.

"They're great, Mom. What cake did you settle on?" asked Valerie. She was getting interested in spite of herself.

"The groom's cake is chocolate marble with a tiny doctor holding a doctor's bag on top," stated Melanie.

"Oh, I love it," said Valerie while Emily smiled and nodded agreement.

"The bridal cake is four tiers. It has flowers all around and the bride and groom on top. The top layer is spice. The second layer is orange. The third layer is butterscotch, and the bottom layer is pineapple," said Melanie.

"Wow," said Valerie. "With all of those flowers on it, it looks gorgeous. Those flavors sound great. I can't wait to dig in."

Marcus smilingly agreed.

"You have outdone yourself, Melanie," said Emily. "That cake sounds like a taste sensation." Melanie flushed with pleasure at all of their praise.

"I told her there was nothing to worry about. I knew you would love all of her arrangements," said Frank.

"I am glad you are here to look over them and I am glad you get to approve everything," said Melanie.

"I absolutely approve everything," said Valerie. "You have done a great job."

"Have you found somewhere to stay tonight?" asked Frank.

"We can check into the boarding house," said Emily.

"Nonsense," said Melanie. "We have plenty of room. You can all stay at the house."

"We don't want to be a bother," said Marcus.

"It's no bother and it's all settled. I won't take 'no' for an answer," stated Melanie.

"Yes, Ma'am," agreed Marcus with a smile.

Melanie reached over and patted his hand. "Let's let the girls know, and we can head for the house and get you settled in," Melanie said in her take charge voice. They all followed Melanie out and headed to the gallery. Emily called her chauffeur to come and pick them up. Melanie explained to Angelica they were leaving and told her if she had any problem Cindy would be there.

"We will be fine. Don't worry," said Cindy. "You all enjoy your visit."

"It was nice meeting you, Angelica," called Valerie as they headed out the door. All of them were chatting with each other. Valerie and Marcus stayed close to each other. They were so in love they had to be in physical contact.

Angelica watched them leave and sighed.

Cindy looked at her. "They are very inspiring," she said. "So are you and Alex."

Angelica flushed slightly. "Alex and I are still getting to know each other," she said.

"Well, good luck to you both. I only hope someday to have what you and Valerie have found. It's very rare and precious." Cindy turned and went to the back room. Angelica stared after her, thoughtfully.

CHAPTER 11

It was only ten minutes to closing time, a week later, when the bell over the door gave a nice tinkling sound. Angelica looked up with a smile. She was surprised to see Stripped Weasel enter. Stripped Weasel approached the counter and gave her a hesitant smile.

"Hello, Stripped Weasel," said Angelica. "It's nice to see you."

"Hello, Little Flower," said Stripped Weasel. "I hope you don't mind my coming by."

"I am very happy you came by. I have always considered us friends." Angelica replied. "What can I help you with?"

"I know it is presumptuous of me to ask, but I didn't know where else to turn," Stripped Weasel looked very uncomfortable.

"Tell me how I can help," said Angelica.

"Do you remember Rose Blossom? Her family is my family's neighbor and Rose was in the same grade as you and me in school," Stripped Weasel stopped and looked at Angelica enquiringly.

Angelica thought for a minute. "Yes, I remember Rose. We were not close friends, but we got along."

"Rose married a man named Gary Long. He was white and they lived here in town. They were very happy and had two children. I was friends with both. Gary worked as a bartender and, six months ago, there was a fight in the bar where he worked. Someone threw a bottle and it hit Gary in the head. He died instantly."

"How awful," exclaimed Angelica.

"Yes, it was, especially for Rose and the kids. They didn't have much insurance and it was mostly used for the burial."

"Why are you telling me about this?" asked Angelica.

"Because when Rose's son; Cole, was visiting his grandparents a few days ago, I saw him outside. He looked so down. I went over and sat and talked with him. It took a while, but he finally told me what was going on. It seems Rose is having a hard time coming up with rent for the small house they are living in. The landlord is hassling her for it. He took her car for two months' rent. And Cole overheard the landlord telling Rose she could pay her rent with sexual favors. She put him off, but Cole is worried about his mom. He is only twelve and he was talking about quitting school and getting a job to help out." Stripped Weasel stopped for breath.

"Give me her address. I will go and talk to her," Angelica handed Stripped Weasel a paper and pen so he could write the address down.

Stripped Weasel wrote on the paper and handed it back to Angelica. Angelica looked at the address and back at Stripped Weasel.

"This is not a very good section of town. I think I had better take someone with me when I go to see her," said Angelica, thoughtfully.

Angelica reached for her phone and called Alex at the hospital.

"Hello, Love," said Alex.

"Hello, Alex." Angelica smiled. "How would you feel about us stopping to see an old friend of mine before we go to eat?" she asked.

"Love to," said Alex. "Do you want to go home first?"

"No, if you pick me up at the gallery, we can make our stop and come back later to pick up my car." Angelica hung up the phone and began to close up so she could leave.

"I'll let you know what happens," she told Stripped Weasel as she let him out of the shop.

Angelica had just finished closing up when Alex tapped on the door. She hurried over to let him in. Alex pulled her close and leaned over for a kiss. Angelica put her arms around him and kissed him back. Alex pulled back and looked at her lovingly.

"Where are we going to visit this friend of yours?" he asked.

Angelica filled him in on what she knew as they drove toward Rose's house.

Alex frowned when he heard how Rose was being treated. "A lot of our girls get into bad situations when they leave the reservation. Do you have any idea about helping her?" he asked.

"I have an idea, but I want to see and talk to her first," said Angelica.

Alex pulled to a stop in front of a shabby house. The yard was well kept, but nothing could stop it from looking shabby. There was a young boy sitting on the porch step. Alex motioned him over.

"Hello, I'm Dr. Steele," he offered his hand to the boy.

"Cole Long," said the boy shaking his hand.

"Well Cole, do you think you could keep an eye on my car while we talk to your mother? I'll pay you five dollars."

Cole looked him over carefully.

"I'll watch your car. You don't have to pay me."

Cole led them up the steps to the front door. He opened the door and stuck his head into the room.

"Mom," he called. "You have company."

"I'll be right there," answered a voice.

Rose entered the room and stopped abruptly when she spotted Angelica and Alex.

"Hello Rose. I don't know if you remember me," said Angelica.

"I remember you," said Rose with a smile. "Welcome home. Hello, Dr. Steele."

"Hello, Rose," Alex responded.

Rose looked enquiringly at the two of them. "Why have you come to see me?" she asked.

"Stripped Weasel told me about your husband. I'm very sorry for your loss," Angelica paused. She was not sure how to proceed.

There was a knock at the door. Rose went to see who was there. She only opened the door a crack. The person outside could not see Alex or Angelica.

"Well, Rose have you thought about my proposal?" he asked

"The answer is 'no.' Just like before, Mr. Clark," answered Rose.

"The way I see it, you don't have a choice. If you want to keep living here," said Mr. Clark. "Do you want to see your kids thrown out on the street?"

Angelica had heard enough. She reached over and pulled the door open and looked at Mr. Clark.

"Hello, Mr. Clark." Angelica gave him her most superior smile.

"Miss Black," stammered Mr. Clark. "I didn't know you were here."

"If this is an example of your rent collection, I think you need to look for another job, one more suited to your personality. Do you have any more business to discuss with my housekeeper?"

He looked from one to the other of them like he was trapped and didn't know which way to turn. He finally looked at Rose.

"Are you moving?" he asked.

"Yes, Mr. Clark. Rose is moving. She will be out by Monday. If anything of hers is touched, the police will be by to see about it. Do we understand each other?"

"Yes, Miss Black." Mr. Clark turned and made a speedy exit. Angelica turned back to Rose

"I'm sorry I didn't get a chance to ask you first. You do want to be my housekeeper, don't you? The job comes with a small house.. It has two bedrooms and a loft room that can be used as a bedroom for Cole. It was a ground keeper's house. I have three of them. I have a big house and I will be hiring more help. I don't expect you to take care of everything by yourself. So, what do you think? You want to work for me?" Angelica paused for breath.

Rose laughed. "Yes, I would love to work for you."

Angelica smiled. "It will be great to have you and your kids around."

Rose looked troubled. "What's wrong," asked Angelica.

"It's just my friend a couple of houses down. She has been having a similar problem with Mr. Clark. Her husband left her for a younger woman. She's been struggling to take care of her two kids. She and I babysit for each other. You did say you were going to hire extra help. Could you try her out and see if she would suit?"

"Tell her to come by the gallery Monday and talk to me. I'll see what I can do. Now, you and your kids get what you want to take with you. We will come back and get the rest later. Your house is completely furnished. We will take you there and get you settled. I have to stop at the gallery and pick up my car and then we will show you your new home."

Alex went outside to keep an eye on his car while Cole went in to get his things.

Angelica came out to talk to him. "You don't mind helping, do you?" she asked.

Alex reached over and pulled her close. "I don't mind at all. I'm very proud of you," he said.

Angelica looked surprised. "I'm just glad I am able to help. Something has to be done about Mr. Clark."

"I agree," said Alex. "It's time he learned to keep his pants zipped."

Angelica laughed at his unexpected bluntness.

"Sorry," said Alex. "I hate when people take advantage of those they have authority over."

Angelica hugged his arm. "I know. I will have to think about what can be done."

They turned as Rose and her two kids came out of the door. They each carried a pillowcase stuffed with their things. Alex opened his trunk and they put the pillowcases in. He then opened the back door of his car and held it while Rose, Cole, and May climbed in.

Angelica led the way from the gallery. Instead of following the drive up to her house, she turned right and followed the road past the garage. After passing the garage there was a small orchard and, between the garage and the orchard, were three houses. Angelica pulled to a stop in front of the first house. Angelica exited her car and went to say hello to Moon Walking, who was waiting in front of the house. While she was giving Moon Walking a hug, Rose and her kids got out of Alex's car and stood looking around.

Rose had tears in her eyes as she looked around at the cozy little house with its flower boxes and colorful shutters. Angelica opened the door and motioned her in while Alex and Cole went to bring in their things. Rose greeted Moon Walking and followed Angelica inside. Alex and Cole came in with their stuff and Angelica showed them where to put the pillow cases. Rose and May followed them around. They were so in awe of everything, they hardly said a word. The largest bedroom was for Rose. They put May in the smaller bedroom next to Rose. They all trooped up the stairs to see the loft bedroom. It was a large spacious room fitted with twin beds and a dresser. The floor was hardwood but there was a large rug between the two beds. Cole had such a huge smile on his face he made them all happy, just looking at him.

They left Cole in the loft to get settled in and went back downstairs. Angelica led them into the kitchen and showed them the well-stocked refrigerator, thanks to Moon Walking.

Angelica showed Rose the phone and the list of numbers on a pad by the phone.

"If you need anything, you just give me a call," she said. "There is a car you can use. I'll have to get the key for you." She opened her purse and took out five one-hundred-dollar bills. She handed them to Rose.

"This is your first two weeks salary. Any food or anything else you need for the house, just ask everyone to send me the bill."

"When do I start work?" asked Rose.

"Next week, after you finish moving. You can start then. I'll be home Tuesday so if you come by the house, I'll show you around. You will need to register the kids in school on Monday." She handed her two more bills. This is to get the kids some uniforms. They have to wear uniforms to school now."

Angelica led the way to the door. After saying goodbye to Rose and May, she, Alex and Moon Walking left the Long family to settle into their new home.

Outside, Angelica turned to Moon Walking. "Thank you for the food. I am glad I don't have to go grocery shopping tonight."

"I was happy to help. Thank you for helping one our families who needed help. The young boy, Cole, is going to be a blessing in the future." Moon Walking told them both good bye and left.

Angelica and Alex smiled at each other and at Moon Walking's cryptic statement. "Let's go home," said Angelica. Alex agreed and they got in their cars to drive to the main house.

CHAPTER 12

They left Angelica's car at her house. Alex pulled it into the garage for her while she went to freshen up before going out to eat.

Alex was waiting for her when Angelica came downstairs. Angelica went straight into his arms for a kiss. Alex pulled her close and kissed her soundly.

When they pulled back, they were both breathing hard. Alex gave her a squeeze and started leading her toward the door. After helping Angelica into the car, Alex rounded the car and got into the driver's seat.

"I think I have worked up an appetite. What would you like to eat?" he asked Angelica.

"I don't care. Anything will do. I have a lot to think about," Angelica leaned back in the seat and thought about all that just happened.

They discussed the problem with Mr. Clark while eating, but they were unable to decide on the best way handle it. Angelica leaned back and looked at Alex.

"Enough about Mr. Clark, I want to enjoy my night with you," she said.

Alex smiled and reached for her hand. "No matter what we are doing, I always enjoy being with you." He leaned over the table and kissed her.

"Ummm," said Angelica. "I think I will have more of that for dessert."

"Let's go," said Alex. "I want to be alone where I can hold you."

Angelica smiled and rose from her seat. She waited while Alex paid the check. They left the restaurant with Alex's arm around her, holding her closely.

Monday was a busy day. Before leaving for work, Angelica took Rose the key to a car in her garage. Rose's friend, Annie Gates, came by and, after talking with her, Angelica offered her the house next to Rose. She was to be on a three-month trial, but Angelica was sure she would be fine. Angelica talked to the mayor, but she was still debating how to handle the Mr. Clark situation.

The gallery was extra busy with all of the excitement of Valerie's wedding. The day was fast approaching and Melanie was very busy with last minute details.

During her lunch break, Angelica decided to stop at the bank and talk to Derrick Bear. No one was at the outside desk, so Angelica knocked on Derrick's office door.

"Come in," called Derrick's voice from inside. Angelica opened the door and peeped inside. Derrick rose quickly when he saw Angelica at the door. "Angelica, it's nice to see you. What can I do for you?" he asked.

Angelica quickly explained about Rose and Mr. Clark. She told Derrick about moving Rose and Annie out.

"I know you have a PI working for you and I was wondering if he could do some investigating for me. I will pay all expenses. I need to know all about Mr. Clark and his family. I want to know who owns those houses and how much they would want for them." Angelica stopped talking and looked at Derrick enquiringly.

Derrick smiled. "I will see what I can find out." He took his phone and placed a call. He gave the PI the information Angelica had just given him. He hung up the phone and smiled at Angelica.

"We should have a report later today or early tomorrow," he said.

Angelica smiled. She stood and extended her hand to Derrick. "Thank you," she said.

Derrick shook her hand. "If you need anything at all, just let me know. I will do all I can to help."

Angelica smiled again as she headed back to the gallery and work.

∽

Melanie was at the gallery when Angelica entered after her lunch break.

"Hello," said Angelica. "How is the wedding coming along?"

"Everything is going smoothly. Valerie will be here on Thursday. She has her dress and we want to go over last-minute details before Saturday. Marcus will be arriving on Friday," Melanie paused to take a breath.

"It sounds like everything is ready," said Angelica, smiling.

"Yes," said Melanie. "If there are no last-minute hitches, we are all set."

"Are there going to be a lot of people coming?" asked Angelica.

"Yes," answered Melanie, "Marcus has invited a lot of friends and acquaintances.."

"Are they going to find places to stay?" asked Angelica.

"Marcus has rented rooms at the boarding house for all of them who want to stay over. Some of them are just coming for the day and leaving early to drive back," Melanie answered.

"Well," said Angelica. "If they need room, I could put up a couple for a night."

"That's very thoughtful of you," said Melanie, giving her a hug. "If we need any help, I'll let you know. I have to get back to it as soon as I talk to Cindy. She is going to be Valerie's Maid of Honor."

Melanie hurried into the back room in search of Cindy. After talking to her, Melanie gave a wave as she hurried out the back door of the Gallery. Angelica went over and checked to make sure the back door was locked.

Angelica smiled as she thought of the upcoming wedding. Marcus and Valerie had been so much in love. Angelica wished the best for them. It always made everyone feel good to see someone so happy. It was quite an adventure the two of them were beginning together.

Angelica thought about Alex. They had become very close in a short amount of time. Angelica knew she was in love with Alex. She just had to wait for him to realize he felt the same way. She could be patient as long as she got to spend plenty of time with him.

Derrick Bear came by the gallery just before closing time. He had a folder for Angelica. "This has all of the information you asked for," said Derrick, handing the folder to Angelica. "If you need anything else, you just let me know."

"Thank you for getting this for me," said Angelica, taking the folder.

"You're welcome," Derrick said as he left the gallery.

Angelica stuffed the papers into her bag and stowed it away to look at later. When she arrived home, Angelica took a shower and freshened up before calling Alex.

"Hello," said Alex absentmindedly.

"Hello," said Angelica. "I just called to let you know I'm at home. You can get back to me when you finish up."

"Angelica," said Alex more alertly. "Don't hang up. I'm almost done. I'll be over in about an hour, if that is okay."

"That is very okay. I'll see you in about an hour."

Angelica hung up phone and retrieved the folder from Derrick Bear. She got herself a glass of tea and sat at the table to look it over.

First was the information on Mr. Clark. He was married and had three children. The children ranged in age from eight to sixteen. His wife worked as a janitor at the elementary school. He owned a modest house in one of the newer subdivisions. Mr. Clark worked for Sun Properties. He collected rent at three housing developments.

Mr. Clark's salary was generous, but any extras were paid for with his wife's salary. The family was comfortable, but they would have a hard time making it without his salary. Angelica frowned. She did not want to hurt his family, but he had to learn to stop harassing the renters.

∼

Alex hung up the phone and turned back to his patient. He found the nurse and interns grinning at him. Even the patient had a smile on her face. Alex ignored the nurse and the interns and smiled at the patient.

"You are doing great, Mrs. Baxter. You should be able to go home tomorrow. I'll leave an order for a relaxant with the nurse and I'll check on you in the morning," Alex reassured his patient. She was an elderly lady and he was very gentle with her.

"Thank you, Dr. Steele. I'll see you in the morning. Enjoy you're evening with your young lady," responded Mrs. Baxter.

"Thank you. I will," said Alex. He gave his patient a smile and left the room. The nurse and interns followed him out. Alex handed the chart, with the new orders on it, to the nurse and, telling the interns good night, headed for his office. In his office he quickly changed his coat, checked to be sure he had everything in order and, after locking his office door, he headed for the parking lot and his car.

Angelica was very important to him. He wondered how long he should wait before telling her he was in love with her. He was determined to ask her to marry him very soon, but he did not want to rush her and take a chance on being turned down.

Alex arrived at his house. He hurried inside, took a quick shower, dressed, and headed for Angelica's place. He was impatient to see her and hold her in his arms again.

Angelica opened the door for Alex and walked straight into his arms. She raised her face for a greeting kiss. Alex pulled her closer and deepened the kiss. When Alex pulled back and looked into her face, they both smiled at each other.

"I've missed you," said Alex.

"I've missed you, too," agreed Angelica. "We just saw each other last night."

"I know," agreed Alex. "Every minute away from you is like a lifetime. I love you."

"I love you, too." said Angelica gazing into his eyes.

"I don't want to rush you," said Alex.

"You aren't rushing me," said Angelica. "I was getting impatient and wondering if you had the same feelings as I do."

"You are the most important person in the world to me. I adore you," whispered Alex.

"Oh, Alex," whispered Angelica. She drew closer for another kiss.

When they came up for air, Angelica pulled Alex into the kitchen. She had food prepared and the table set attractively. She told Alex to take a seat while she got their drinks of iced tea.

CHAPTER 13

"What's this?" asked Alex motioning to the folder of information at the end of the table.

"It is information Derrick Bear compiled for me on Mr. Clark and the housing development. I asked him to see what he could find out," said Angelica.

"Is there anything interesting?" asked Alex.

"I only just started reading it. I put it aside to prepare dinner. I thought we could look it over together after we eat," said Angelica.

"Okay," agreed Alex. "This food is delicious. Thank you for cooking. You didn't have to. We could have gone out."

"I know. I felt like staying in. I didn't want to share you with anyone else tonight," Angelica reached over and squeezed Alex's hand.

Alex squeezed her hand back and smiled. He leaned over for a quick kiss, before going back to eating. He didn't let go of her hand though.

After they finished eating, Alex helped Angelica clear the table and load the dishwasher. They returned to the table to look over the papers from Derrick Bear. Angelica handed the profile on Mr. Clark to Alex.

Alex frowned as he read about Mr. Clark's family. "I think I have had Mrs. Clark as a patient. She had an accidental chemical burn from work. It wasn't very bad. She was treated and sent home. She seemed like a nice lady. I hate how her husband is treating her."

"I hate it, too. There should be a way to stop him without hurting his family," said Angelica.

They took the other papers out. They were about the rental properties. The properties were about to be condemned because they were in such bad shape. The health department decided they were a health hazard. The city was studying the situation.

"What will happen to all of those families if the properties are condemned?" asked Angelica.

"The city will evict them. They may offer them alternative housing, but most of the families will not be able to afford the higher rents," said Alex.

"I could probably buy the property for almost nothing. I could improve the houses one at a time and move the families to the improved houses before starting on the vacant houses. Do you think I am being unrealistic to think about taking on this project?" asked Angelica.

"No, I think it is a very workable idea. There are some contractors on the reservation. Their work has been slow. They would do good work and keep an eye on Mr. Clark. You need to talk to someone with the city and see if they will be behind the project. You don't want to be condemned before you get started," said Alex.

"I'll call Derrick tomorrow and ask him to deal with the city. As soon as I get the go ahead from him, I'll talk to Moon Walking and ask her to recommend some contractors." Angelica paused for a moment.

Alex was still looking at the papers. He looked startled as he read the names of the property owners. "I know one of the owners. I'll call him tomorrow and sound him out about selling you the property. They should be ready to sell at a rock bottom price. After all, they are about to be condemned." Alex concluded grimly.

"Thank you," said Angelica. "You don't mind me doing this, do you? After all, with us together, it will be your headache, too."

Alex put an arm around her and pulled her close. "I love you. I love that you are trying to make it better for so many people. I will be right there with you all the way. Anything you need from me I will try my best to supply whatever you need."

Angelica pushed the papers aside and stood. She sat in Alex's lap and put her arms around him. "It's going to be the two of us all the way. Without you, life would have no meaning. Without you, I would have no joy in this new life that I have been given. I believe I was sent to you because we are meant to be together. I love you. You are my other half."

Angelica and Alex came together in a passionate kiss. After a few minutes, they came up for air.

"Angelica," said Alex. "Will you marry me?"

"Yes," said Angelica.

Alex reached into his pocket and pulled out a ring box. He opened it up and took out a beautiful star sapphire ring. He then took Angelica's hand and placed the ring on her finger.

"Oh!" exclaimed Angelica. "It's beautiful. When did you get this?"

"I got it a couple of days after you arrived from the past. I knew we were meant to be together, and I wanted to be prepared." Angelica sank into his arms for another kiss. "Moon Walking is going to be happy. All of her predictions are coming to pass," said Alex.

"I don't care. I love Moon Walking, and I love that she is going to be my Grandmother," said Angelica.

Angelica leaned back and closed her eyes. "Moon Walking," she thought to herself. "Alex just asked me to marry him, and I said yes."

"Good," answered Moon Walking. "Tell him I am happy he is showing such good sense. Welcome to the family, Little Flower."

Angelica opened her eyes and smiled at Alex. "Moon Walking said to tell you she is happy you are showing such good sense. She also welcomed me to the family."

Alex looked at her wide-eyed. "You can talk to Moon Walking?"

Angelica nodded. "Yes, she said for me to practice and I would be able to talk to you, also."

Alex smiled. "We will practice. I think I will love being able to hear you without others hearing."

"It does sound like fun. Nobody will know we are talking to each other," Angelica laughed softly.

"As much as I hate to let you go, we both have to work tomorrow," Alex hugged her close and kissed her again.

When the kiss ended, Angelica stood up and pulled Alex up by his hand.

"I don't care if we do have to work tomorrow. I am not ready for this night to end." She led him toward the living room and the sofa. She sat down and motioned for Alex to join her.

Alex sat down behind her and pulled her close. He leaned back on the cushions and pulled her closer in his arms. He rested his chin on the top of her head and savored the feel of her in his arms.

Angelica snuggled into Alex's arms and lay her face on his chest. She could hear his heart beating. It seemed to be beating a little fast.

"I love you," she thought.

"I love you, too," Alex answered in her mind.

Angelica looked up at Alex and smiled. "We did it," she said.

"We did what?" asked Alex.

"We talked in our minds," said Angelica.

Alex looked startled, then, he smiled. "I didn't even realize we were not talking out loud."

Angelica lay her head back on his chest and snuggled. "I knew we were perfect together," she said.

Alex smiled. "Yes, we are a perfect match."

CHAPTER 14

Angelica called Derrick Bear before she went in to work. She had his cell phone number from the card he enclosed in her bank papers. She told him about the property which was on the verge of being condemned. She asked him if he could talk to someone in the city department and feel them out about her buying the property and fixing it up. Derrick assured her he would make some calls and get back to her. She thanked him for his assistance and hurried to get to work.

Alex called the man whose name he recognized from the report. When they first started talking about the property, the man talked about putting a larger price on the property. Alex reminded him of the pending condemned designation facing the property. He also told him about the good publicity they would get from turning the property over to the Black foundation. He explained about the renovations and helping the people stay in affordable homes. The man agreed. He said he would talk to the other owners, but he was sure they would agree to turn over the property to the Black foundation. The foundation would probably only have to pay closing costs, lawyer fees, and property taxes. Alex thanked him and hung up the phone.

Angelica had just entered the gallery when she received the call from Alex. "Hello, Alex. Did I tell you how much I loved waking up in your arms this morning?" said Angelica.

"I believe you mentioned it a time or two," smiled Alex. "I just got off the phone with one of the property owners. He has to talk to his partners, but he thinks he can get them to agree to turning the property over to the Black foundation for the payment of all closing costs, lawyer fees, and property taxes."

"Oh, Alex, this is really going to happen!" exclaimed Angelica.

"It looks like it," said Alex. "Did you talk to Derrick?"

"Yes, he is going to talk to someone and get back to me," said Angelica.

"I'll see you after work. I love you," said Alex.

"I love you, too," agreed Angelica.

"What's all the excitement about?" asked Cindy coming out of the back room.

Angelica explained to her about the property and her plans. While she talked, she moved her hands around excitedly. Cindy's eye focused on the ring on her finger.

"I think it is great helping all those families, but is that what I think it is on your finger?" she asked.

Angelica smiled and showed her ring to Cindy. "Yes, Alex and I are engaged. He asked me last night and I said yes," said Angelica.

"It's beautiful! Congratulations," said Cindy. She gave Angelica a hug. "I wish all the best to both of you."

"Thanks," replied Angelica.

Cindy and Angelica turned to the door as Melanie entered, followed by Valerie and Frank. Cindy drew their attention to Angelica's ring and there were oohs, ahhs, hugs, and congratulations all around.

Angelica then told them about the housing project. They were happy someone was trying to help the people struggling to survive.

"You're not going to leave us, are you?" asked Melanie. "I really enjoy having you around and you have been a great hit with the customers."

"No," said Angelica. "I love working here. When things get started, I may have to take time off sometimes to see to things, but I plan on hiring competent people to handle things for me."

"Good," said Melanie. "Now, we need to get the gallery open and Valerie and I need to get to work on the wedding."

She, Valerie, and Frank went into Frank's office after congratulating and hugging Angelica once again.

"I need to get to work, too," said Cindy.

She went to the back room. Angelica went to the front to open the gallery and prepare for customers.

Angelica was practically floating on air. She was so happy. The housing project was coming together and she was so in love with Alex. She was beaming at the customers so much they started smiling back at her. They all seemed to be happier when they left the gallery. The sales were up remarkably.

Derrick called during lunch break. He confirmed the city was willing to go along with anything the Black Foundation wanted to do. They would even give them tax exemption status until the renovations were complete. After the renovations were finished, the property would be given a reduced tax rate for the next ten years.

"Wow," said Angelica. "I'll get my lawyers on the project today. Alex has talked to one of the property owners and I can probably get the property for closing cost, lawyer fees and taxes."

"Great," replied Derrick. "If there is any way I can help, just let me know."

"I will. Thanks so much for all you have done. As soon as I close on the property, I will talk to Moon Walking about hiring some native contractors for the renovations," said Angelica.

"There are good contractors on the reservation. They will be glad for the work, and they will do it well," said Derrick.

"Yes, Alex told me about them. Thanks for calling, Derrick. I'll be in touch. I have to get back to work. I'm working extra to help Melanie while she is preparing for Valerie's wedding."

"Alright, let me know if there is anything else I can help with," said Derrick.

"I will." replied Angelica as she hung up the phone.

Angelica called Alex and filled him in on her conversation with Derrick.

"Great," said Alex. "The owner I talked to about the property just called me back. He said the other owners were ready to go along with the deal. So, everything is working out."

"I'll call the foundation lawyers and get them working on everything. We should have it all settled by early next week. We will have this weekend clear to go to Valerie and Marcus' wedding," said Angelica.

"Yes," agreed Alex. "Then we can begin working on our wedding. I do not want a long engagement. I miss you when I can't touch you."

"I don't want a long engagement, either," replied Angelica. "I want us to be together, too. After all, the universe sent me to you. Who are we to argue with the universe when it decides it is love's time?"

Alex smiled. "I would never argue with the universe, especially, when the universe is sending me my heart."

"Oh, Alex!" exclaimed Angelica tearfully. "I had better go back to work before you make me cry. I love you. I'll see you after work."

"Bye, Love," said Alex.

They both hung up their phones and went back to work.

Melanie came through at closing time. She told Angelica they decided to close the gallery until Monday so they could concentrate on the wedding. She had a sign to put in the window. It read, "Closed for Valerie's wedding. Open on Monday, regular time." She took the sign and placed it in the front window.

"Is there anything you need me to help with?" asked Angelica.

"No, everything is in order. Just show up at the church at two o'clock Saturday," replied Melanie.

"I'll be there," smiled Angelica as she gathered her purse and prepared to leave.

She and Melanie left by the back door. Melanie locked up behind them and they went to their separate cars.

Angelica pulled out her phone to call Alex.

"Hi," she said when he answered. "Melanie just put a sign in the window saying we are closed until Monday."

"Great, I'll see if I can get someone to cover for me tomorrow. I would love to have the whole weekend with you," replied Alex.

"That would be great," said Angelica.

"I'll see what I can do and meet you at your house as soon as I can," said Alex.

"Okay," agreed Angelica. "I love you."

"I love you, too," said Alex. He hung up the phone and went in search of someone to cover for him the next day.

CHAPTER 15

Angelica stopped to talk to Moon Walking on the way home. She found her at her house. It was unusual to find her at home. She was almost always out and about. They greeted each other with a hug. Moon Walking invited her in and offered some ice tea.

"I would love some ice tea," said Angelica. She waited until Moon Walking brought two glasses in to the front room and sat down. She brought Moon Walking up to date on the property deal and about needing the native contractors.

Moon Walking nodded her head. "I was talking to Standing Elk yesterday. He said that building is slow right now. I told him not to worry, work was coming. He seemed reassured," said Moon Walking.

"Standing Elk, is he kin to Laughing Elk?" asked Angelica.

"Yes, he is his uncle. Laughing Elk works for him," replied Moon Walking.

"Laughing Elk is the one who brought my attention to the trouble Rose was having. He was trying to help her and her kids. I think he feels close to her son," said Angelica.

"It is good for them both to help each other. Laughing Elk is missing his son, since he has started at the university, and Cole misses his father," said Moon Walking.

Angelica nodded her head in agreement. "I need to get home and start dinner," said Angelica. "I'll see you Saturday. You are going to the wedding with us, aren't you?"

"Yes, thank you, I would be glad for a ride," said Moon Walking.

Angelica gave Moon Walking a hug. "I'm glad you are going to be my grandmother. I have always felt like you were my family." Angelica gave Moon Walking another hug and started to leave.

Moon Walking reached over and took her hand. "Little Flower, I have known since you were a baby you will always be very important to me and my family. I am glad you and my grandson are making it official," Moon Walking hugged her and then stood watching as Angelica drove away.

After Angelica arrived home, she showered and went to see what she had for dinner. She had just started looking when the doorbell rang. Angelica closed the refrigerator and went to answer the door.

She opened the door to Alex. He leaned over and kissed her, but it was a brief kiss because his hands were full of boxes of food.

"What's all this?" asked Angelica with a smile.

"This is dinner. I didn't want to go out and I don't want to spend any time watching you cook. You are beautiful when you cook, but I have other things on mind for the evening. I want to hold you in my arms, so lead the way to the dining room," said Alex.

Angelica laughed delightedly and turned to go to the dining room. Alex followed closely behind her. He piled the boxes on the table and turned to Angelica. He gathered her into his arms and greeted her properly.

"Hello, love," he said, still holding her close.

"I like the way you say 'hello,'" said Angelica. "What kind of food did you bring? I am starved and it smells great."

"I brought Chinese. I hope you like it. I should have called you first and asked, but I was driving by the place and stopped on impulse," replied Alex.

"If it tastes as good as it smells, I will love it," stated Angelica.

Angelica got out plates and forks. While Alex put food on the plates, Angelica brought the pitcher of iced tea and two glasses to the table. They then sat down and dug in.

"Umm, this is good," said Angelica. "You can impulse buy for me anytime." She smiled lovingly at Alex and continued to enjoy her meal.

After they finished and put away the leftovers, Alex pulled Angelica into his arms. "I want a proper hello," he said and proceeded to kiss her passionately. Angelica cooperated fully. When they finally pulled back slightly to breathe, Angelica laid her face on his chest.

"Hello," she said. "You want to go out and come in again so we can say hello again?"

Alex laughed. "Why don't we just say 'hello' again without me having to take my arms from around you?"

"Okay," agreed Angelica. They spent the next minutes saying a very passionate 'hello.'

When they stopped for breath, Alex led her to the sofa. After sitting down, he looked down into her eyes. "When can we get married?" he asked.

"I don't know," said Angelica. "We have Valerie and Marcus' wedding this weekend. Are we getting married on the reservation or in church?"

"We can do whichever you want, or both if you want to," said Alex. "Derrick Bear is an ordained minister. He is also a justice of the peace. So, if we want to have our ceremony on the reservation, we can get him to preside, and it will be legal in both cultures."

"That sounds wonderful. How about two weeks from Saturday. We can check with Derrick and be sure he doesn't have any conflicts. We can get time off for a honeymoon, and I'll have time to get my project up and running. I also need to buy a dress," Angelica paused for breath.

"I'll get started on the arrangements in the morning. I can't wait for us to be together," said Alex.

"Where are we going to live?" asked Angelica.

"I thought we could live here. We can put my house up for sale or find someone who needs it and let them live there rent free. They would have to pay the utilities and I could keep an eye on the place," said Alex.

"Oh, Alex, what a wonderful idea!" she exclaimed. "I know interns have a hard time finding housing when they start out, and it is close to the hospital, but you would have a longer drive to work and back."

"As long as I know you will be here to come home to, the drive is unimportant. I love you. I can't wait to have you as mine," said Alex.

It was quite a while before they did any more talking.

Saturday dawned as a beautiful day. Alex and Angelica went by and picked up Moon Walking. Together, they headed for the church.

"Hello, Moon Walking," said Angelica. "How are you?"

"Hello, Little Flower," replied Moon Walking. "I am good. I am looking forward to your and Running Wolf's joining. Do you need any help getting ready?"

"I would love having your help. After all, you are my grandmother now," said Angelica.

Moon Walking smiled with satisfaction. Alex and Angelica smiled at each other as their hands came together.

They entered the church and were escorted to their seats. There were a lot of people there already. Angelica smiled and nodded to the ones she knew. There was a group of people she didn't know. She spotted Marcus' mother in the group so she thought they were friends and family of Marcus.

They took their seats and waited for the wedding to begin. The preacher appeared at the front and then Marcus and his best man came out to stand at the side by the preacher. The music started and they turned to watch Cindy walk toward the front. There was another bridesmaid being escorted by a groomsman next. The music changed and then Valerie appeared, being escorted by her father. Everyone stood while the glowing bride was led to the front by her father. Frank kissed his daughter's cheek and placed her hand in Marcus' hand. He then took his seat by Melanie.

The preacher went through the vows, getting the appropriate

answers, from Valerie and Marcus. It was soon over and the couple confirmed their vows with a kiss. The preacher introduced them as Mr. and Mrs. Marcus Drake. Everyone stood as Marcus and Valerie walked down the isle. They were followed by Cindy, the best man, the bridesmaid and her escort. Everyone else followed. They arrived outside to see Valerie and Marcus leaving in a limo to go to the country club for the reception. They all piled into their cars and followed.

At the country club they were introduced to The Grey and Jenkins families. It turned out that Valerie's bridesmaid was Malinda Grey, and her escort was her husband Daniel. Valerie and Mallie had become friends.

Valerie and Mallie, each with their husbands in tow, came over to speak with Moon Walking. Valerie thanked her for coming and gave her a hug. Valerie turned to Marcus.

"Why don't you guys wait here with Alex while us girls find the ladies room?" asked Valerie. After getting a nod from the guys, Valerie led the way to the ladies' room.

The girls headed to the mirrors and started checking their makeup. Moon Walking took a seat on the large sofa.

"It was a beautiful wedding," said Angelica.

"Yes," agreed Moon Walking. "Things are as they should be. You all are united with your intended mates.

"Yes," agreed Mallie. "Most people don't believe when they find out Daniel and I met while we were in a coma.

"I know," agreed Valerie. "Most people think I am kidding when I mention Marcus and I met in a dream."

"Well," said Angelica. "I have an even stranger tale. I was sent twenty years into the future to be with my love."

"You all are very lucky. The universe put you together with your proper mates. Always be thankful for fate's intervention," said Moon Walking.

"We are very thankful," all three girls agreed, smiling at Moon Walking.

"We had better get back before three impatient men come looking for us," said Mallie.

They walked toward the door and all three stopped and smiled. There, standing by the wall, were Marcus, Daniel, and Alex. Each of the ladies fell into the arms of their respective partner. Gazing into each other's eyes they kissed. .

"It is as it should be," said Moon Walking. "This is love's time."

The End

ABOUT THE AUTHOR

With five children, ten grandchildren and six great- grandchildren I have a very busy life, but reading and writing have always been a very large and enjoyable part of my life. I have been writing since I was very young. I kept notebooks, with my stories in them private. I didn't share them with anyone. They were all hand written because I was unable to type. We lived in the country and I had to do most of my writing at night. My days were busy helping with my brothers and sister. I also helped Mom with the garden and canning food for our family. Even though I was tired, I still managed to get my thoughts down on paper at night.

When I married and began raising my family, I continued writing my stories while helping my children through school and into their own lives and families. My sister was the only one to read my stories. She was very encouraging. When my youngest daughter started college, I decided to go to college myself. I had taken my GED at an earlier date and only had to take a class to pass my college entrance tests. I passed with flying colors and even managed to get a partial scholarship. I took computer classes to learn typing. The english and literature classes helped me to polish my stories.

I found public speaking was not for me. I was much more comfortable with the written word, but researching and writing the speeches was helpful. I could use information to build a story. I still managed to put my own spin on the essays.

I finished college with an associate degree and a 3.4 GPA. I had several awards including Presidents list, Deans list, and Faculty list.

The school experience helped me gain more confidence in my writing. I want to thank my English teacher in college for giving me more confidence in my writing by telling me that I had a good imagination. She said I told an interesting story. My daughter, who is a very good writer and has books of her own published, convinced me to have some of my stories published. She self published them for me. The first time I held one of my books in my hands and looked at my name on it as author, I was so proud. They were very well received. This was encouragement enough to convince me to continue writing and publishing. I have been building my library of books written by Betty McLain since then. I also wrote and illustrated several childrens books.

Being able to type my stories opened up a whole new world for me. Having access to a computer helped me to look up anything I needed to know expanded my ability to keep writing my books. Joining Facebook and making friends all over the world expanded my outlook considerably. I was able to understand many different lifestyles and incorporate them in my ideas.

I have heard the saying, watch out what you say and dont make the writer mad, you may end up in a book being eliminated. It is true. All of life is there to stimulate your imagination. It is fun to sit and think about how a thought can be changed to develop a story, and to watch the story develop and come alive in your mind. When I get started the stories almost write themselves, I just have to get all of it down as I think it before it is gone.

I love knowing the stories I have written are being read and enjoyed by others. It is awe inspiring to look at the books and think I wrote that.

I look forward to many more years of putting my stories out there and hope the people reading my books are looking forward to reading them as much.

Lightning Source UK Ltd.
Milton Keynes UK
UKHW010954280820
368951UK00004B/151